TORMENT
By H E Joyce

With grateful thanks to my editor: Elaine Denning.

Cover by The Cover Collection.

Contents

One

Two Months Earlier

The basement room was dimly lit. It was dank, soundproof, and far from earshot of anyone. Besides which, the woman was strapped securely into a chair in the middle of the room, her mouth taped. Nobody would hear her stifled, terrified pleas for help.

The only source of light was a small desk lamp on the table in front of her. It pointed directly at her so she could see nothing through the glare of the light. Classical music played mournfully on a loop, the sound filling the room from speakers in every corner. The woman's eyes were wide with fear as they scanned the dark recesses; beads of sweat dotted her forehead and cheeks as she struggled in vain to release herself from the chair.

Occasionally she would catch an almost ghostly glimpse of a dark figure in one shadowy corner of the room one moment and in another corner the next. And so it went on, until eventually the suited man silently approached from behind and slowly began to remove the tape from her mouth.

'You must promise to be a good girl and not to scream. Do you promise?' he said calmly and emotionlessly.

The young woman nodded furiously and he pulled the tape completely away.

He leaned down and spoke softly into her ear. 'That's good,

that's very good. Now, tell me again, what is your fear?'

'I – I – I, please no, no more, please, I beg you.'

'Come now my dear, you have to play the game – you know the rules. How can I help you if you won't abide by the rules?'

'Please, just let me go. I won't tell anyone, I promise you.'

'No, of course you won't, I know that. This is our little secret – correct? And of course, it's all for the greater good, you do know that, don't you my dear?'

'Yes. Yes I do – for the greater good. I know that now.'

The man nodded. 'That's good. That's very good. So, you are going to join us in our work, is that correct?'

'Yes, yes, I'll join you.'

He looked at her thoughtfully. 'I'm sorry my dear, but I'm afraid I don't believe you. Now then, let me ask you again. What is your fear?'

'You know what it is.'

'Yes, but that's not how we play the game, is it? You have to tell me – so tell me – what is your fear?' he said, backing away into the shadows once again.

'I won't do it, not anymore. Just let me go and you'll never see or hear from me again. I give you my word.'

He emerged from the dark again, appearing behind her. He rested his hands on her shoulder for a moment. 'Suffocation! That's your fear, isn't it?' he said, calmly pinching her nose and covering her mouth with his free hand.

He grinned with delight, lost in the moment, as the life drained from her.

Two

Present Day

The grey stone building was drab and badly run down, yet it was an imposing structure. Like so many other institutions of its kind, no money had been spent on it for years. Dulled, ageing paintwork was peeling away from the window frames and doors and, in places, ivy crawled up the walls unchecked. The only positive that Helen could see was the spectacular location. Bad enough if the hospital had been on the outskirts of some equally miserable town, but no, The Manor Psychiatric Hospital was situated in open Lake District countryside, miles from anywhere or anyone. Even so, on such a day as this, wet, grey and harsh, as many days were in the Lake District, it did not take on the appearance of a place conducive with recovery.

It was the middle of October and raining steadily as she drove her Ford hatchback into the hospital grounds. It was raining in the same steady, relentless way as it had the first time she had visited six weeks earlier, and now, as it had then, the place filled her with an irrational sense of foreboding. She had worked in hospitals, which had been low security facilities; she had coped well with the patients and never once had she let anything get to her. The Manor was a medium security hospital and there was a feeling about the place she could not put her finger on. Nevertheless, as she parked her car, she dismissed her unreasoned thoughts, putting them down to first day nerves in a new job, with new colleagues, and in a part of the country that was virtually unknown to her.

Helen was a psychiatrist and the post was a residential one. She would work normal hours but be on call at night. Her line of work was demanding, both physically and mentally, but despite her slight build she had proven herself more than physically capable. Also, she was not prone to nervousness amongst patients, something that some people found to be a problem and could never get past. It was the undoing of many a career. Helen, at thirty-two, was more feisty than her five-foot, six inches declared. She was slim, unassumingly attractive with wavy, shoulder length hair of deep red, and had, in the past, shown more spirit and fortitude than many of her peers.

She parked her car in a visitor's space just outside the main reception, took a deep breath and went through the automatic sliding glass doors. Behind the plate-glass reception was a sullen woman with short, straight grey hair and a round face of pale complexion, wearing glasses that only went to heighten her severe look. She continued flicking through pages of a book for what seemed to Helen a very long time before eventually looking over the top of her glasses, unsmiling at Helen as she stood patiently waiting.

'Yes, can I help you?'

'Yes, I'm Helen Ross, I'm the new Doctor who's starting work today, and I believe I'm supposed to report here.'

'Oh? Well, let's have a look then, shall we?' She searched through a disorganised array of papers strewn across her desk.

Eventually, she dug something out. 'Yes, here we are. Ross, you say?' the woman said, unimpressed.

'Yes, that's right.'

'Take a seat over there,' she said, pointing to the far side of the reception, 'someone will be along shortly to sort you out.'

'Thank you.' Helen looked around for a moment. 'Is there a coffee machine, by any chance?'

'No, afraid not. Suppose I could make you one if you like.'

Helen smiled. 'Only if it's not too much trouble, it's just that I've been driving for a long time – I'm gasping.'

The woman nodded. 'Well, sit down over there and I'll bring some over when I get a moment.' She picked up the phone, dialled a number and stared at Helen as she waited. After a few moments her call was answered and she spoke in a hushed tone, still staring across at her. The conversation was brief; she then stood up and disappeared around a corner. A faint whooshing sound told Helen the woman was boiling a kettle.

The reception area was clean and, she supposed, recently decorated, quite deceptively pleasant and modern in comparison to the Victorian exterior. There were four doors leading off the reception, one into the receptionist's office and three others that led into corridors that branched off like a rabbits warren, leading to doctor's offices, wards, living quarters and therapy rooms. It struck her now, as it had previously, that, for such a facility, it was strangely quiet and tranquil.

A short while later, the woman reappeared. 'Wasn't sure how you liked it, so I made it white, no sugar.'

'That's fine, thanks, uh... sorry, I don't know your name.'

'Mary,' she said curtly.

'Well, I'm pleased to meet you, Mary. Have you been here long?'

'Long enough,' she said, dispassionately.

It was clear to Helen that the woman had no desire to engage in conversation so she simply smiled, took a sip of her coffee and said, 'well, thanks again, it's much appreciated I assure you.'

The expressionless woman said nothing but simply turned on her heels and returned to her desk, head down, seemingly working, though occasionally Helen caught her looking up and glancing fleetingly in her direction. It wasn't often that Helen took an instant dislike to a person, she was, after all, a people person, someone who liked to get on with others. She was always prepared to give a person a second chance, however her first impression of Mary was that there seemed precious little to like.

Helen glanced at the clock mounted on the wall above the receptionists head, then instinctively at her watch, which she knew was correct. It had just turned 8.30am and still there was no sign of a staff member coming to greet her. She put her coffee down on the table amongst a scattering of magazines and approached the woman behind the plate glass. 'Excuse me; I assume somebody does know I'm here?'

The woman looked up slowly with a disdainful expression. 'Yes, they know, someone will come for you soon. My, we are eager, aren't we?'

'I'm sorry?' Helen said, irritated. There was no response

from the woman and Helen chose not to pursue it further. Instead, she turned away and returned to her seat. She had barely sat down when she heard someone tapping a code into the security lock of the door and then a buzzing sound as the electronic catch released. It was a relief to see the senior psychiatrist appear, though he looked somewhat flustered.

Helen raised herself from her seat as he approached. He was a short, slightly built man in his late fifties, completely bald and sporting a tweed jacket and bow tie. He smiled a smile that looked obligatory rather than natural, like someone who had just received bad news but was putting a brave face on.

'Doctor Ross, hello, I'm so pleased to see you. Did you have a good journey?'

'Hello Professor Kirkby, yes, a little tiring, but not too bad, thank you.'

'I take it you've met Mary. Has she been looking after you? I must apologise for having kept you waiting so long.'

'Yes, we've met, and she was kind enough to get me some coffee, so…'

'Good, good,' he interrupted. 'Well, first things first, let me show you to your office, then we can get you introduced to the staff,' he said, once again tapping the code into the door. 'After that, you can move your things into your personal quarters and settle in; we won't expect you to work on your first day.'

'Oh, I don't mind starting straight away,' Helen said eagerly.

The professor placed a hand on her back and tapped it lightly. 'I admire your enthusiasm, but I think it would be best if you start work in earnest tomorrow. Besides, it'll take you a day or so just to find your way around and get to know everyone. Don't worry, your patients can wait one more day, they're being well cared for, I can assure you.'

Helen nodded. 'Well, of course, if that's what you want.'

'It is,' he said, a hint of authority in his voice. He laughed it off. 'The senior members of staff always have lunch together, it will give you a chance to get to know everyone better and, of course, sample the delightful cuisine on offer.'

'I can't wait.'

'Oh, it's not as bad as you might think, in fact it's very good,' he said, as they continued walking along the corridor, 'and I'm sure you will get along excellently with your new colleagues. They're a fine bunch of people, very dedicated – as I have no doubt you are, Helen.'

She felt a blush creep into her cheeks. 'I'll try my best not to disappoint you, Professor Kirkby.'

'I'm *quite* sure you won't, Helen – *quite* sure.'

The corridor, with its many wards off to each side, seemed never ending, but eventually reached a point where it branched off to both left and right. Nursing staff passed them along the way, but apart from that, it still seemed eerily quiet.

Professor Kirkby came to a halt. 'Now, your office and treatment room is along here on the west wing, come along.'

It was dark in comparison to the main corridor, only a few fluorescent lights lit the way, some flickering intermittently. Lime green paint adorned the walls and ceiling; there were no windows, no natural light.

'Well, here we are; this is your office.' He unlocked the door, then handed her the key. Helen entered and was pleasantly surprised to find a bright, well-appointed office and to her relief, a window that looked out onto a grassed courtyard.

'It's very nice,' she said.

'I'm glad you like it, we've had it redecorated especially for your arrival. Your treatment room is right through there,' he said, pointing to a connecting door. 'As you will see, your case notes are on your desk. Do you have any questions before I leave you?'

'You're leaving? I'm sorry, but I thought you were going to introduce me to the other staff.'

'Well, time is getting on,' he said, glancing at his watch. 'I think it would be best to leave the introductions until lunch. We eat at 1pm. Now, if you go back the way we came, you'll find the dining hall along the east wing corridor about a hundred yards or so.'

'Okay, and my living quarters?'

'Yes of course, I'm sorry, I completely forgot about that. I'll get someone to show you to them after lunch, if that's alright.'

'That's fine, Professor,' she said, walking around her new desk and idly perusing the case files. 'I'll see you at lunch then.'

'I look forward to it,' he said, and with that he left.

She took a look around her office, delighted and surprised to see in one corner of the room an espresso machine; what's more, it was an identical model to the one she owned. She wasted no time in getting it working.

A few minutes later she sat back in her brand new office chair and savoured the rich, black coffee. Looking out to the courtyard she saw that it was still raining, if anything more heavily than before, and just for a moment, yet not really knowing why, a slight sense of despondency crept into her thoughts. Just tiredness, she supposed, trying to shake off the morose feeling.

The stack of case files on her desk beckoned her; her mind needed a distraction. She took the top one and opened it, skimming only the basic information at this stage: name of the patient, diagnosis, the treatment administered so far, and any progress made. She then moved onto the next case until eventually the stack had been transferred from the right of her desk to the left. The similarity in each case was striking. She had immersed herself so deeply that the morning had come and gone.

She had just finished when the phone rang; she physically jumped. It was Professor Kirkby. 'It's 1.15; can we expect the pleasure of your company for lunch, Helen?'

She flicked her eyes up at the wall clock, amazed at how quickly the time had passed. 'Uh, yes, I'm sorry Professor, I had no idea it was that time already. I'll be right there.'

'Thank you, that would be most splendid,' he said, with what Helen thought was a hint of sarcasm.

Even at this early stage, she wasn't sure if she liked him.

Three

The staff dining room was unlike anything she had seen of the hospital so far, it was more in keeping with the building with its oak panelling, plush carpet and large open fireplace. A long walnut dining table, the veneer surface slightly dulled and cracked in places, stretched out in front of the fireplace and towards one end sat the small group of white-coated senior staff members with Professor Kirkby seated at the head of the table.

He pushed his chair back and stood as Helen entered. Those sat with their backs to the door turned, unsmiling, to regard their new colleague. Professor Kirkby on the other hand approached her with a cheery smile and guided her to a place set to his left at the table. She took her seat with all eyes on her. The uncomfortable silence in the room was broken by Professor Kirkby.

'Firstly, let me introduce you to everyone,' he said, gesturing to his colleagues in turn. 'Sitting next to you is Doctor Wright, and then we have Doctors Schmitt, Brownlow and Gregory, Sister Thornton, and lastly, Doctor Scott.' In turn they all nodded silently.

'Pleased to meet you all,' Helen said, 'I'm looking forward to working with you.'

'Right, well now you're here we can start our lunch,' said Professor Kirkby.

Helen looked around the table at the untouched meals. 'Oh,

I'm sorry, I had no idea you were waiting for me.'

Professor Kirkby gave a wry smile at his colleagues. 'Well, it's just as well we have cold meat salad today, isn't it?' He paused for a moment. 'Of course, we do try to make it to meals on time here, Helen. Just to say that perhaps you could bear it in mind. Anyhow, *please*, enjoy your lunch.'

Helen didn't quite know how to take him; he could seem charming one moment and sarcastic the next. She took it as a rebuke from someone who clearly liked to run a tight ship and feel in complete control of his staff, even if it meant embarrassing them in public.

It was not the way she liked to work. Had she ever needed to reprimand anyone in the past, she had always done so quietly and privately. She didn't care for his cynical, publically mocking approach, and particularly to a new member of a team. Was it so important to be on time for lunch? Indeed, was it so important that the staff had lunch together at all? Sometimes, often in fact, in her previous job, she never managed to have a lunch break. It all seemed so trivial somehow.

'So, Helen, what have you been up to, to distract you so much?' he asked.

'Oh, you know, just going over my case files.'

He paused for a moment, his fork hovering half-way to his mouth. 'Really? We *are* keen aren't we?'

'Well, that's why I'm here after all – to do a job,' she said, meeting his gaze. 'I think it's important to get to learn something of one's patients as soon as possible, wouldn't you agree?'

'Yes, of course, it's really most admirable. And did you?'

'Did I learn anything? Yes, a little I think.'

'Good! Excellent! he said, his eyes darting nervously at the others, and always it seemed to Helen, with the same forced smile. He did not pursue it any further, but ate his forkful of food and proceeded to cut through the thick piece of ham on his plate.

'What made you decide to come all the way here, to work in our humble establishment? I understand you're from London, is that correct?'

Helen looked across at Doctor Brownlow, seated opposite her. 'I really wanted to get out of London. I always feel it's good to experience new challenges throughout ones career, don't you?'

He was a distinguished looking man in his mid-forties, with dark hair and a touch of grey at the sides. 'Yes, absolutely,' he said, 'it just seems so far to come. Do you have family in these parts?'

'No, no family. Both of my parents have passed away and I've no brothers or sisters, so there was nothing to keep me there. London's great, but it can be such a lonely place and I've always loved this part of the country, so here I am.'

'Well, I'm sure you'll prove to be a great asset to us,' Professor Kirkby interjected.

Helen smiled. 'I'll do my best not to disappoint you, Professor.'

'Of course,' said Sister Thornton, a hard faced woman in her fifties, 'you may find we do things a little differently here. I hope you are a person who can adjust to change.'

Helen glanced at her. 'Yes, I think so, though surely your practises can't be that different? I mean, there are standard guidelines – still, I'll be in your hands.'

'Yes, that's quite correct,' she said coldly, and stared down into her plate.

Helen shrugged. 'Well, I'm always eager to learn new techniques.' She poured herself a glass of water and, out of the corner of her eye, she could see Professor Kirkby looking over the top of his glasses and listening with interest as he continued to eat. She regarded the others sat around the table. All except for one was eating, a fairly young doctor of a similar age to her. She was, like Helen, quite small but with short black hair that was undoubtedly dyed, a pale complexion and large, steel blue eyes, heavy with makeup.

She sat almost slouched at the table, looking up only once with hostility, sadness, or despondency in her eyes. Helen could not decide which. She only ever moved her food around her plate with a fork, stabbing at the cold meat and potatoes, but never actually eating anything, and although Helen would have liked to, she did not attempt to engage her in conversation. Similarly, the other members of the team showed no interest in conversing further with Helen, or anyone else for that matter, they simply ate their lunch in subdued silence.

Helen turned to Professor Kirkby. 'When will I be able to see my patients? I'd like to get to work as soon as possible, if that's alright?'

The professor sighed. 'Helen, Helen, Helen, as I said earlier, there's no rush, it's all covered for today, you can start work tomorrow. In the meantime, I suggest you get settled into your living quarters and just rest. You've had a long journey. Your eagerness to start work is admirable, but I'd prefer to have you fresh and alert, so for today, just relax.'

'Yes, of course,' she said, 'if that's what you want.'

Professor Kirkby, with a single nod of agreement, smiled almost imperceptibly.

'Well, in that case, you won't mind if I go to my car and get my things,' she said, raising herself from the chair.

'Helen! Please – sit.' His voice hinted at annoyance. 'Kate will show you to your quarters after lunch. What's your hurry?' he said, 'we still have dessert to come; I believe today it's apple pie with custard – my personal favourite, and after that, coffee. As I indicated before, we take lunch together here – I believe it's important we all spend time together away from our work.'

Helen took her seat again, not unlike a scolded child. He may have been a small, insignificant looking man, but his manner was intimidating. She felt it in the air, and the apparent, silent conformity of the others at the table bared testament to this.

As the dessert arrived, Professor Kirkby looked disapprovingly at Kate Scott as her plate was removed, the food barely touched. 'Not hungry again, Kate? You know you really must try to make an effort to eat something, besides, you know how I feel about wastefulness.' The young doctor said nothing; she just shrugged her shoulders slightly, like an admonished teenager.

Helen smiled at her as their eyes met momentarily; she was pleasantly surprised when the young doctor, albeit faintly, returned the smile. Unsure quite why, Helen felt sorry for her; she looked like a fish out of water, unhappy and lonely. Perhaps, in time, she thought, they might become friends.

It seemed that Professor Kirkby was the only one in the group with what you would call a healthy appetite and, as he skimmed the last remnants of custard clinging to his dish, whereas everyone else had hardly begun their dessert, he sat back in his chair contented, but looked around at all the full dishes as if he could still eat more.

'So, Helen,' he said, turning to her. 'You say you've been studying your case files. Find anything of interest?'

'Well, I only glanced at them really – nevertheless, it did occur to me that very little progress, if any, seems to have been made with *any* of them over the last few months.'

His face was stern. 'I don't need to tell you, do I Doctor, that psychiatry is not an exact science. There are many variables and unknown factors, and…'

'Yes, of course, I realise that, Professor Kirkby, and I don't want to speak out of turn, but given the time that most have been here, I would have expected to see at least a *little* progress.'

He gave her a sardonic smile and laughed a little as he spoke. 'You're clearly very thorough, Helen, it must have been something more than a glance, I suspect.'

She shrugged. 'I just wanted to know a little about my patients, that's all.'

'Most commendable, but let's not forget that the kind of psychosis your patients suffer from is extremely tricky and unpredictable. No one can wave a magic wand and cure them just like that. And yes, there will be times when a patient slips back…' he paused for a moment, 'however, we keep trying, don't we?' he concluded.

Helen guessed she had flustered him, and simply answered, 'Yes, I suppose we do.' Perhaps he was not used to such straight talking from his staff. For the first time he had let his guard slip and showed frustration at being out talked. Out of the corner of her eye, Helen could see a broad grin growing on Kate's face, though she attempted to conceal it from Kirkby and the others with her hand discreetly across her mouth. Helen decided to push the envelope a little further as the coffee arrived.

She rose from her chair. 'If it's alright with you, I think I'll skip coffee. Is that alright?'

'Yes, yes, please, carry on,' the professor said. The arrogant grin had disappeared now. Helen knew she had won a little victory. 'In fact, Doctor Scott can go with you; she can show you to your living quarters. *If* that's alright with you?' he said sarcastically.

'Yes, well that would be great, that is if Doctor Scott doesn't mind, of course.'

Kate could not have made it clearer that far from minding, she was relieved to be excused. Before Helen knew it, Kate was by her side, smiling, as if rescued from a terrible ordeal. By way of reasserting his authority, Professor Kirkby called out to Helen as the two reached the door.

'Oh, and Doctor Ross – dinner is at eight sharp.'

Helen looked at Kate a little open-mouthed and smiled as she turned to Professor Kirkby.

'Eight sharp – right!'

Four

'Is he always like that, Kate?' Helen asked, as they walked the corridors.

'Yes, he is I'm afraid, or worse. It was great to see you stand up to him like that; everyone else is scared to death of him, him and that awful Doctor Wright. It'll be good to have someone to talk to at last.'

'How long have you been working here?'

'About a year, but believe me it seems much longer.'

'Yes, well I can kind of understand that. Do you live in?'

'Uh huh, my rooms are just a few doors away from yours. I suppose after a while you'll be looking for property in one of the nearby villages.'

'Maybe,' Helen said, 'but not right away. That's quite a big step and I'm not so sure I want to commit myself just yet – I'll just have to see how it goes.'

'Well,' Kate said, with a hopeful smile, 'I hope you do decide to stay. The place isn't so bad when you get used to it.'

'No, I'm sure it isn't,' Helen said sceptically.

'No – really, it isn't, you'll see. Well, here we are, this is your place, that's mine over there. The others have living quarters at the other end of the building.'

'Are you telling me that all the staff live-in?'

'Yes, that's right,' she said. 'You can bring your car around to unload your stuff whenever you like, there are parking spaces just outside.'

Helen pulled down on the handle, pushed the door open and went inside. The heavy curtains that were drawn closed made the room completely dark. She pulled them open to reveal a small, fairly basic living area. She opened a door and glanced in at what was the bedroom, then the bathroom. There was no kitchen, no facilities for catering for oneself.

'What do you think?' Kate asked.

'Well, it's not exactly the Ritz.'

Kate chuckled. 'Can you find your way back to the main reception and your car okay, or would you like me to take you? It's just that, well, I should really be getting back to work.'

'No, you go, I'll find my way somehow,' Helen said, casting her eyes over the drab, magnolia paintwork. 'Thanks Kate. I'll see you at dinner.'

'Eight sharp!' Kate called out as she disappeared along the gloomy corridor.

'What the hell,' Helen muttered to herself. 'Yes, eight sharp!' she shouted, then said under her breath, 'I can hardly wait.'

She looked around the impersonal room that would, at least for a while, be her home and then went into the clinical looking bedroom which comprised a single bed, wardrobe and bedside table. Clinical it may have been, but as she looked around her the surroundings seemed unimportant as she realised quite suddenly how tired she was.

The bed beckoned her. She lay down on top of the crisp, white sheet and conceded that Professor Kirkby may have had a point after all; that it might, as he had strongly suggested, be best to start work tomorrow when she was rested and reinvigorated.

As she lay there, feeling a delayed fatigue from her journey, she felt her eyes becoming heavy. She closed them and drifted inexorably into a fitful sleep. The dreams followed; nightmarish images of Professor Kirkby and Doctor Wright filled her mind. Her body flailed and writhed, twitched with anxiety, until she woke with a start; the phone by the bedside was ringing with a shrill, annoying tone that caused her to sit bolt upright. She was perspiring.

She glanced at her watch before answering, and although it felt only like a matter of minutes that she had been asleep, an hour and a half had passed. An amber light on the phone winked persistently in unison with the ringing. She composed herself and picked up the receiver.

'Hello, Doctor Ross speaking.'

'Ah, Helen, it's Professor Kirkby. I hope I didn't disturb you. Were you sleeping?' He didn't wait for an answer. 'Anyway, I was wondering if you would mind joining me in my office for a moment. I won't keep you long.'

'Uh, yes, of course. Is something wrong?'

'No, I'd simply like to introduce you to a patient – one of *your* patients, in fact. She's having an episode and I thought it would be useful for you to see it.'

'Yes, okay, I'll be right there,' Helen said, rubbing her eyes. 'So, your office you say, and where...?'

'Follow the signs, you'll find it. As quickly as you can please,' he said, with a superior tone and an unnatural, almost unnerving composure that his voice always seemed to convey.

Helen hurriedly pulled on the white coat that had been left for her, hanging wrapped in polythene on the door, complete with an identity badge already pinned to it. As she left her room and made her way down the dimly lit corridor, she thought to herself what an odd character Professor Kirkby was. At lunch he had seemed set against her becoming involved in work in any way at all on this, her first day. Now, he called for her, knowing fully well she would not be prepared. His ways, his manner, and possibly his working practices, would take some getting used to, she thought. Nevertheless, she was very familiar with the idiosyncrasies of fellow psychiatrists and she was quite certain she could cope with one more.

She realised, when she'd pulled the self-locking door shut, that in her haste she had left her key on the bedside table of her room. There was no time to worry about it; she would, in all probability be able pick up a spare from reception later. It also occurred to her that having fallen asleep, she had not yet got her few possessions from the car and unpacked them. It was uncharacteristic of her to be so lapse or to tire so easily during the day. Yes, it had been a very early start. And yes, it had been a long drive, yet she couldn't help feeling she hadn't got off to the best start.

Making a fresh start in a new hospital, with new colleagues, and in a part of the country where she knew no one was always going to be risky. At her old hospital in London, she had been very highly thought of by her colleagues, both junior and senior. Now it was a case of starting from scratch, and with Professor Kirkby, it seemed to her it would be a hard and bumpy road if she were ever to gain his respect.

Helen walked briskly along the corridor. There was no natural light, only the cold, dim glow of fluorescent tubes every few yards, some faltering and flashing intermittently on the ceiling. Her room was situated almost at the very end of the corridor, so she knew the direction she was walking would eventually lead her back to the main hospital building, the reception area, and hopefully signs pointing the way to Kirkby's office. Failing that, she supposed, she could always ask that most friendly of receptionists, Mary, whom she'd met earlier that day.

There was an oppressive, dismal feel to the corridor so she quickened her pace again in order to reach the natural light and, as she did so, the clicking of her heels echoed all around her. As she rounded a corner, she could see and hear human life in the reception - an orderly escorting a patient, the sound of the switchboard buzzing, and light; wonderful daylight.

The few minutes' walk had seemed to take an age and a feeling of great loneliness and despair had seemed to ooze from the very walls. It felt good to be in the relative comfort of the reception area once again. Helen glanced at Mary behind her glass window; the woman looked up with a disdainful sneer. Looking at the various signs situated above the two remaining corridors, Helen was relieved to see one for Professor Kirkby's office. She would not have to throw herself at the mercy of the inimitable Mary after all.

Helen strode across the reception, all the time sensing the receptionist's eyes following her. She flung the swing doors open and proceeded down the equally dismal corridor that led to a number of wards, a day room, and ultimately to Professor Kirkby's office. It was as she neared the day room that a young woman, Helen guessed around twenty-six, bare-footed, dishevelled, unwashed and in a nightdress, emerged. She stood in Helen's path staring vacantly at her, her head drooping forlornly towards her shoulder. There was nothing unusual about the patient's behaviour, Helen simply smiled and side-stepped to continue on her way.

The woman, with lank strands of brown and blonde streaked hair stuck to her face, blocked Helen's way and pushed herself close, grabbing hold of her arms, and peered into Helen's eyes pitifully.

'Get me out of here – please, help me, I can't stay here,' she said, with surprisingly good articulation. Again, this was by no means unusual behaviour. Although, in this case, Helen thought she detected something in her voice, she wasn't sure what – but something, perhaps genuine fear of something – or someone.

'Try to stay calm. What's your name?' asked Helen.

'Maria – my name's Maria. You have to help me.'

'Okay Maria,' Helen said, taking her by the arm, 'I can't stop now, but I promise I'll come back and see you in a very short while. Is that okay?'

'You promise?'

'I do. Now, you go back in there,' she said, leading her to the day room, 'and try to relax. I'll see you soon.'

The woman said nothing, but obediently did as Helen asked. At the door, she turned to Helen again. 'You're new, aren't you? You've no idea what's going on here – but you will.'

Helen looked at the woman quizzically and proceeded along the corridor. Professor Kirkby's office was at the very end; she paused, then knocked on the door.

'Come!'

Helen entered the office to see the professor standing in the middle of the room in discussion with a sister. They both turned their heads briefly as she entered but continued talking, this time almost in a whisper. Helen stood awkwardly, looking around the office as she waited for them to conclude. The patient she was supposed to meet was not evident. Had he summoned her there on a wild goose chase – on a whim?

His office was spacious and lavishly decorated with heavy, dark velour wallpaper in parts, whereas other sections of the walls were oak panelled. His desk was situated by a large window with extensive views of the grounds and the surrounding hills and countryside beyond. Their conversation complete, the sister looked scornfully at Helen and turned to leave.

'Oh, by the way, this is Sister Thornton, Helen,' said Kirkby.

The woman simply nodded without taking the hand that Helen offered. She then left.

'Well, Helen, I'm afraid you got here a little late. I sent your patient back to the ward. No matter, I'm sure you have a good reason for taking so long.' He looked at Helen as if waiting for her reason.

'I can only apologise, Professor. I got here as quickly as I could. I can't have been more than ten minutes, I…'

'No matter,' he interrupted, sitting down behind his desk. He gestured silently for Helen to sit opposite him, then leaned back in his chair, linked his fingers and rested his chin on them. 'What happened?' he said calmly.

'What happened?' Helen enquired curiously.

'Yes, I was wondering what might have kept you from getting here sooner.'

'Well, as I said, I was only...'

'I don't wish to chastise you on your first day, Doctor Ross, but I do insist that when I call a member of staff to my office, they turn up promptly – do you understand?'

Helen hesitated for a moment, slightly bewildered. 'I apologise Professor. As I said, I...' she broke off, believing that an excuse, whatever it might be, was not something he would tolerate. 'Yes, I understand,' she said.

'Good! Well, I won't keep you. You may return to... well, whatever it was you were doing.'

'Right,' she said, slightly confused. 'And the patient you wanted me to see, do you mind me asking who it was and what happened?'

'We can discuss it another time, tomorrow perhaps, once you start work properly. Now, if you'll excuse me,' he said, picking up a pen and shuffling some papers on his desk.

'Of course, I'll see you at dinner then.' Helen rose from her chair and Kirkby merely grunted, put on his half-framed glasses, and buried his head in his paperwork. Clear there would be no further reaction from the professor, and once again puzzled by his behaviour, she left saying nothing more.

True to her word, once out of Kirkby's office and making her way along the corridor, she diverted into the day room to find the woman who had seemed so distressed. There were a handful of patients wandering aimlessly around the room. Chairs regimentally lined the outer edges of the room, but none were occupied. A nurse sat at a work station in one corner reading a magazine, but there was no sign of Maria.

Helen went unnoticed by the nurse as she approached, even when she reached the woman's work station. She stood over her and feigned a cough to get her attention.

The nurse looked startled and quickly closed her magazine. She looked Helen up and down for a moment before speaking.

'I'm sorry, I was just taking a short break, you must be the new doctor. I hadn't realised you'd started yet – Doctor Ross, isn't it?' she said, peaking at Helen's name badge.

'Officially I have, but on Professor Kirkby's orders I start work properly tomorrow.'

'I see. What can I do for you?'

'I met a patient in the corridor earlier, her name was Maria; I told her I would call in to see her. Do you know where she is by any chance? It was only a few minutes ago.'

'Yes,' the nurse nodded, 'you've just missed her; Sister took her back to the ward.'

'I see. Which ward is she in, do you know?'

'Ward ten. I believe that's the ward that you'll be in charge of, isn't it? I wouldn't try to see her just now though, she's a little upset and Sister wouldn't like it.'

Helen studied her curiously. 'Oh?'

'I think she was going to sedate her, you see.'

'Okay, well thanks anyway. What's the patient's surname, do you know?'

'I believe its Dobson, yes that's it, Maria Dobson.'

'Thank you. Well, I'll let you get back to your break,' Helen said, with a hint of sarcasm.

She couldn't be certain, but Helen thought it was very likely that Maria Dobson had been the patient she had been summoned to see by Kirkby. But why would he and the sister change their minds so quickly and have the woman removed from his office? She wondered if, perhaps, there had been something they didn't want her to see or hear.

Five

The whole episode had been bizarre. Firstly, Kirkby summoned her to his office on the notion of meeting one of her patients. Secondly, once she had arrived, and in Helen's opinion at least, not late, the patient was no longer there. And thirdly, after all that, he refused to discuss the patient or the reason for calling Helen in the first place. It seemed to her that the man was something of an enigma. In fact, out of all the members of staff she had met so far, Kate appeared, relatively speaking, to be the only normal one amongst them.

One thing was clear: Kirkby's word was law and he was not going to be an easy person to work with. Not that having a head of staff running a tight ship was something she was against, on the contrary, but in her experience there was a way of doing so in a more human and less overbearing manner.

Had she made a terrible mistake leaving her old job? She hoped not. She had loved working there, but apart from escaping the city, there had been another reason for the new start – Peter. He was a senior clinical psychologist at her old hospital in London, and they had been having an affair for around a year. The only problem was that he was married. To complicate matters more, his wife was also a doctor at the same hospital. She and Helen worked together closely at times, she always seemed nice and, unfortunately, Helen liked her.

Peter had told Helen he would divorce his wife so that they

could get married, but the guilt was too much. As much as she loved Peter, if his marriage was destined to break up she had no desire to be the one who caused it. It would have been easier had his wife been a malevolent person, someone who was easy to dislike – but she wasn't, and Helen decided after much soul-searching that the only decent thing she could do was end the affair.

That, of course, had brought its own problems. The tension between her and Peter had become palpable. Something had to give; it ended with Helen resigning once she had secured her new post at The Manor. She had tried to keep her resignation secret but somehow, as these things always do, it got out.

Peter begged her not to leave, saying he couldn't bear it, not seeing her each day, but Helen was adamant and told him it was for the best. She didn't tell him where she was going, only that she was moving away from London. And now, here she was, in a part of the country and in a new hospital where she knew no one, and she couldn't help feeling a little scared.

Even as she approached the reception desk she felt apprehension. However, she was pleased to see that the sullen face of Mary had been replaced by a far cheerier face, someone with an actual smile.

'You must be Doctor Ross,' said the woman, cheerily.

'That's right. Mary not around?'

'No, you've just missed her. We change shifts at four, you see. Did you want to see her about something? Or is there something I can help you with?'

'Well, it's a little embarrassing, but I've locked myself out of my room. I was in a bit of a rush and left my key behind.'

'That's not a problem,' the woman said, delving into a drawer behind her desk, 'here's a spare one. Just drop it off when you've finished with it – no hurry.'

Helen smiled, taking the key. 'Thank you, you're a lifesaver.'

'Not at all, only too pleased to help – especially for a newcomer. I'm Kathleen, by the way.'

'Helen,' she said, reaching out to shake the woman's hand. 'It's good to see a friendly face.' She turned to leave, then paused, looking back at her. 'By the way, what are the patient visiting hours? It seems very quiet; I haven't seen a soul all day.'

The woman looked baffled for a moment. 'Visiting times? Well, we don't really seem to have any visitors here.'

Helen looked at her curiously. 'What, none?'

'Well officially, we do of course have visiting times, but the thing is, none of the patients seem to have any. I never really gave it too much thought before, but now you mention it, it is quite strange.'

'Yes, it is – very. Well, thanks Kathleen, I'll drop the key back later, okay?'

'No problem,' she called out, as Helen left, this time by the main entrance.

The rain had diminished to a light drizzle. Helen got into her car and drove it round to the back of the building, hoping she could find the entrance that led to her room. Her car contained all her worldly goods: clothes, some personal effects, and a few pieces such as table lamps and other decorative items to brighten up her small living quarters. The flat she had rented in London came already furnished so, physically at least, it was a very easy move to make. Emotionally? That was another matter.

She managed to find the isolated area at the rear of the grounds where her room was situated, parked close-by and, piece by piece, removed her belongings from the car and made her way through the door that led into the corridor. It took only around twenty minutes and as soon as she had finished, the first thing she did was plug in and fill her coffee machine. It was the one possession she couldn't live without.

There was a lonely, solitary feeling to the zone that would be her home for months or perhaps even years. The silence was overwhelming and along with the greyness outside her window, as well as the drab, clinical interior, it made her feel quite morose.

After the machine had worked its magic, she poured herself a large cup of cappuccino and took it into the bedroom. She propped herself up on a pillow and savoured it, before setting the alarm on her mobile phone for 7pm. There was time for a short nap before getting ready for dinner. Not that she was at all hungry, nor did she particularly relish the company of Kirkby or his bunch of sycophants. All she really wanted was to sleep until the morning – that however, clearly wasn't an option, not tonight.

Nevertheless, she thought to herself, she would have to face the professor at some point and make it perfectly clear to him that she would, when she so desired, miss dinner in favour of relaxing in her room, or even going out to a local pub to eat instead. If no one else had the guts to stand up to him, then she would. He had no right to expect that of his staff and she for one would not stand for it.

The thoughts running through her head made her angry; she could feel her heart rate increase. Then she went over what the receptionist, Kathleen, had told her, that there were never any visitors for the patients. The veins in her temples began to throb; she no longer felt relaxed enough to sleep – or was it simply the coffee, or perhaps even first day nerves?

The loud knock on her door startled her and she jumped, just avoiding spilling coffee down her front. She lowered her feet reluctantly from the bed and slipped her shoes on as the door was knocked again, this time with more vigour. 'Yes, I'm coming, I'm coming,' she called out irritably.

'Hi!' Kate said, over-cheerfully as Helen opened the door.

'Hi, what's up?'

'Nothing, I just thought I'd check on you, you know, see that you'd settled in okay.'

'I'm fine,' Helen said flatly, 'a little tired after my journey, that's all. It's been a long day, but other than that... would you like a coffee? I've just made some.'

Kate shook her head. 'No thanks, I've got to get back. I'll be finished in an hour though. I just wanted to know you were okay. You don't mind do you?'

'No, of course not. It was very considerate of you.'

'Oh that's good, because I really do want us to be friends, Helen. Well, I'll leave you to it and see you later then.'

Helen shut the door, relieved to have a little more time on her own, and decided it was as good a time as any to unpack her clothes and assorted knick-knacks. Even if she had still felt like sleeping, there would, she thought, judging by the afternoon so far, be little point in trying. She made herself another cup of cappuccino in the hope it would keep her awake long enough to get through dinner that evening. As far as she was concerned, the sooner it was over and done with the better. All she really wanted was a good night's sleep, to meet her patients, and get down to some real work the next morning.

∞∞∞

Helen was unpacked, showered, and dressed by 7.45pm. It was then that Kate knocked on her door and Helen braced herself for an hour or so of the professor's and his strange associates' company. If they were as quiet and subservient as they had been over lunch, with Kirkby dominating the conversation, the evening would indeed seem a long one. She made certain to grab her room key and the spare before answering the door.

The smile had gone from Kate's face; she seemed more serious, more intense than she had been earlier that afternoon, and more like she had been over lunch.

'I didn't want to rush you too much, but I thought I should give you a knock. We don't want to be late,' she said nervously.

'That's okay, don't worry. Look, I'm ready,' she gestured, wiggling her key, 'we've plenty of time.'

'Yes, I suppose so; it's just that it puts him in such a foul mood if anyone isn't on time.'

'So I found out this afternoon,' Helen said. 'Still, I may have something to say about that. Free time is free time and I won't be dictated to in how I use it. Do you never miss dinner? I mean, aren't there times when you go off the hospital premises for dinner – to a local pub, something like that?'

Kate looked visibly shocked. 'No, never,' she said, as they briskly walked the corridor, 'he wouldn't like that one little bit.'

'Yes, well, we'll have to see about that, won't we?'

Kate frowned. 'You're not thinking of taking him on, are you? He has a terrible temper, you know.'

'I've no doubt he has, but he can't interfere with his staff's private lives, that's just wrong, and the sooner he realises that the better for everyone. Don't worry, I can handle him.'

'I hope you're right. But he's not a bad man really, you know, just a little eccentric, that's all.'

'Look, don't worry; I'm not going to go in both barrels blazing. I can be very diplomatic when I need to be. I'm sure he'll see reason. He has to.'

'I suppose you're right,' Kate said, reservedly.

'I think it will be good for everyone to have things shaken up a little around here. If lunch was anything to go by, almost the entire staff seems downtrodden and lacking morale. It also strikes me as being very strange that all of them are residential – no offence.'

'That's okay, none taken,' Kate said, stopping at the dining hall door. 'Maybe better not to say anything tonight though, eh?'

Helen smiled wryly. 'Maybe, we'll see.'

It was 7.55pm when the two entered the dining hall. Kirkby and all the other staff were already sat at the table. Kirkby rose from his chair momentarily, slowly clapped his hands, and smiling, said: 'Helen, you made it – congratulations.' The others around the table looked on without expression or emotion, all except for the sister, sitting at Kirkby's side, who smirked at his comment.

His sarcasm did not amuse Helen though; in fact she was seething inside. She bit her tongue, saying only, 'good evening' before taking her allocated seat at the table.

'Dinner will be served shortly, Helen. I hope you're hungry, it's a hearty casserole tonight, I believe,' Kirkby said.

'Sounds good. Yes, I'm sure I can manage to eat something.'

'Good, I like my people to have a healthy appetite. It's not only good for the body, but also the mind, don't you agree?'

'Yes, absolutely.' She paused for a few moments and then continued. 'Though, I think there are many other factors to keeping the mind healthy that are just as important.'

'Such as?' enquired Kirkby, reluctantly.

'Oh, well, I'm sure there's no need for me to tell *you,* Professor.'

He raised an eyebrow and leant forward on the table. 'Indulge me, Helen.'

'Well, the mind needs rest – proper rest. At other times it needs stimulation – stimulation other than work, I mean. Outside stimulation, variety, seeing different people. Otherwise it will simply stagnate. But you didn't need me to tell you that, did you?' she laughed.

'Quite so, but forgive me, I can't help feeling that you're trying to make a point, Doctor.'

'No, I'm simply answering your question,' Helen said, pouring some water into her glass.

'I see,' he said, pulling at his bow-tie uncomfortably. At that point the catering staff brought in the first course of their meal. It was a welcome distraction for Kirkby. As for Helen's co-diners, it also appeared to be a timely entrance; Helen could clearly see the relief on their faces. It seemed to her they did not welcome confrontation. Or more disturbingly, were they somehow afraid of it?

Six

To the relief of many, including Kate, the evening passed without any further hint of disagreement. Helen had made a point of not provoking or being provoked into debate. In fact, as at lunch, it had been a quiet affair. It was unnatural, but on this occasion it suited Helen quite well. She suspected it had also suited Kirkby. She slept well that night, and woke refreshed and eager to begin work.

It was 8am and, after a quick cup of coffee in her room, she made her way to her office and immediately started to peruse the patient notes once again. The previous evening over dinner, Kirkby had told her that there was to be a general staff meeting at 10am in his office, and determined not to be a second late, she set the alarm on her mobile for 9.45am, just in case she became too immersed in reading the case files as she had the previous morning.

She unlocked and opened the desk drawer where she had placed the files. This time though, her fingers came into contact with something tucked away deep at the back of the drawer. She pulled out the files, then reached in again. It was clearly a book of some description, possibly forgotten by her predecessor. It was a desk diary with several elastic bands wrapped tightly around it, seemingly for some kind of naïve security. She counted ten altogether. Whomever it belonged to, and she could only imagine it to be that of her predecessor, was showing classic signs of paranoia.

It did not feel right somehow, but she reluctantly opened the diary. She found that the last entry was made in August. What immediately struck Helen was the erratic handwriting; it showed signs of a deep anxiety, concern, possibly even fear by its author. It wasn't until she actually read the entry that she realised how right she was, the distress in the barely legible scrawl was intense and real.

As she flicked through the pages, it quickly became evident it was not a personal diary as such but a recorded account regarding patients and the practises at the hospital. She could scarcely believe what she was seeing and returned to the final entry. The doctor indicated that she had witnessed enough and was about to blow the whistle on Professor Kirkby and some of his associates.

Helen looked up from the book and sat dazed for a moment. 'What have I got myself into?' she murmured to herself. Why hadn't she heard of, or seen any damning reports about the hospital when she had looked at applying for the vacant post? Deep in thought, it was at that moment Kate entered the office. She hadn't knocked and it took Helen by surprise. She furtively covered the diary with some papers.

'Hi, just thought I'd drop in to remind you about the staff meeting at ten. I'm sure you haven't forgotten, but... Anyway, did you sleep well last night?'

'Uh, yes, thank you, I did.'

'Are you okay? You look like you've seen a ghost,' Kate said.

'Yes, absolutely, I'm fine.'

'Okay, well I'll see you there then. Don't be late, will you?'

'Don't worry, I won't be late,' Helen said, a hint of exasperation in her voice. Kate smiled sheepishly and left. 'Damned meeting! When are they going to let me get to work?'

She looked through her stationery drawer and pulled out a large envelope, placed the diary in it and walked over to her filing cabinet. She then put it at the very back of the bottom drawer where no one would be likely to find it. It seemed the concept of privacy around The Manor was unheard of and positively discouraged by Kirkby. Secrecy on his part, however, was a different matter entirely. At least that's how it appeared.

∞∞∞∞

Helen silenced the reminder on her mobile, took a last mouthful of coffee, locked her office door and made her way to Kirkby's office. She passed the ward where she had encountered the agitated patient in the corridor the previous day. She peered in as she passed, but saw no sign of her; however, she fully intended to see her once the meeting was concluded.

She knocked on his office door as a matter of courtesy; Doctor Brownlow opened it with a reserved smile and wished her a good-morning. The rest of the staff were already in attendance and sat around Kirkby's desk, blankly looking around as Helen approached to take a seat.

'Good-morning, Doctor Ross. I trust you had a restful night?' said Kirkby.

'Good-morning. Yes I did, thank you.' She took her seat between Doctor Brownlow and the stern female doctor, Eva Wright.

'Well, everyone,' Kirkby said, looking over his glasses, 'who would like to begin?' He broke off to speak directly to Helen. 'Doctor Ross, I should explain, we have these meetings every morning to discuss any matters arising regarding patients. We like to keep it informal.'

If that were the case, it would be the only thing that *was* informal, Helen thought. 'I see,' she said.

'Of course, as you haven't yet seen any of your patients, we won't be expecting any input from *you* today. Still, it'll give you an idea of what the meetings are all about, won't it?'

'Well, as a matter of fact, I did briefly meet one of my patients yesterday – when I was on my way to your office. She seemed extremely agitated; I'll be seeing her later.'

Kirkby looked at Helen thoughtfully. 'Yes, well as you might be aware, Doctor Ross, this happens to be a psychiatric hospital. I think it's safe to say that agitation in patients is to be expected – wouldn't you agree?' he said with a grin. Muted laughter emanated from the others as one by one he looked at them expectantly.

'Yes, I am aware of that, Professor.'

His grin immediately disappeared. 'And might I enquire who the patient in question is?'

'Maria Dobson.'

'Oh, Maria,' he sniggered unsympathetically. 'I don't know what she said to you, but let me assure you, agitation is nothing unusual with Maria. She's suffering from delusional fantasies and acute paranoia. For now, I suggest you simply continue the treatment of your predecessor.'

'Thank you, Professor, I'll certainly bear that in mind.'

'Good – then shall we continue?'

He addressed each doctor in turn, asking if there were any issues that needed to be discussed regarding any of their patients. The answer was always the same – nothing, everything was fine. Was everything fine? Helen doubted it. More likely they were telling him what he wanted to hear. Maybe they were simply too afraid.

The meeting was brief. 'Well, if there's no other business, let's go to work people, and I'll see you at lunch.'

The doctors began to raise themselves as Helen spoke again. 'There is one thing I would like to ask.' Everyone looked at her and lowered themselves again. Kate looked positively nervous.

Kirkby stared at Helen with a look of frustration. 'Please, go ahead,' he said, leaning his chin on entwined fingers.

'I'm told that none of the patients have any visitors. I was wondering why that was? Just seems a little odd, that's all.'

'Yes, you were informed correctly,' he said, glancing accusingly at Kate, 'but I can assure you the explanation is quite simple. It's just that, as it happens, none of our patients have anyone *to* visit them.'

'No family *or* friends?'

'Apparently not, no.'

'I see – how odd,' Helen said sceptically.

Kirkby simply shrugged and said, 'so, is that it? Or does anyone else have any questions?' He waited for a moment.

'Good, alright then ladies and gentlemen, in that case I'll see you later.'

They all stood to leave, including Helen.

'Doctor Ross, if you wouldn't mind, I'd like a word.'

Her heart sank. Now what? she thought. A pep-talk, perhaps, because she had dared to ask questions?

'Please, sit,' he said. 'I won't keep you from your work long, I'm sure you're eager to start. I was wondering how you were settling in. Is your accommodation to your liking?'

'Yes, it's fine.'

'Any concerns?'

She thought better of saying any more at this stage. 'No, nothing, but then I've only been here a day.' She paused for a moment. 'However, this might be a good time to tell you that I won't be joining you and the other staff for dinner tonight.'

His eyes widened. 'What? What do you mean, you won't be joining us?'

'I'll be going out for dinner this evening. There's a nice little pub about six miles down the road, I passed it on the way here yesterday. I thought I'd give it a try.'

He had clearly had the wind taken from his sails. 'But – but we always dine together, that's the way it's always been, Helen. At least, as long as I have been in charge. No, it's simply not on, I'm afraid.'

She smiled out of disbelief. 'Are you forbidding me to go out and do as I please during my own free time, Professor?'

'I –I.'

'Look, if you want my opinion, well – I just don't think it's healthy, and I'm sorry, but I'm afraid I *will* be going out this evening. After all, I'm a doctor, not a patient.' Kirkby appeared shocked at her outspokenness. She waited a moment before continuing; wondering if he had a rebuttal, but none came. 'Well, if that's all, Professor, I would like to get to work now.'

He again said nothing, but with a flick of his hand gestured that she was free to leave. She rose and walked out of the office with a slight smile of self-satisfaction, although in a way she felt sorry for him. Perhaps the obsession with having his staff around him at meal times was born from loneliness. Nevertheless, she knew she was right in standing up to him on the matter. She was fairly certain, also, that there would be other confrontations with him along the way. It seemed somehow inevitable.

∞∞∞∞

Helen immediately made her way to the day room where she had briefly met Maria the day before. She scanned the room but among the half-dozen or so patients there was no sign of Maria Dobson. Some of the patients seemed unaware of her presence, indeed unaware of anything; others stared into space with a vacant gaze. The nurse in charge approached her. She was a middle-aged woman, fairly plump with short, blonde hair that was just beginning to grey.

'Good-morning. Doctor Ross isn't it? I'm Staff Nurse O'Callaghan. Can I help you?' Her manner was matter-of-fact although pleasant enough.

'Yes, how do you do,' Helen said, shaking her hand. 'I was

looking for a patient of mine, Maria Dobson, but she doesn't appear to be here. I take it she'll be on the ward.'

'Not exactly. She's on a side-ward at the moment.'

'I see, well I'll pop along and see if I can find her.'

'Yes of course, although I believe she's quite heavily sedated.'

'Hmm. Well I'll have a chat with the ward sister. Thanks anyway.' Helen glanced at the handful of patients who were dotted around the room. 'Are any of these patients mine, by the way?'

'Yes, a couple of them, there's Judy over there, the one looking out of the window, and Samantha, sitting at the table holding the same cup of tea she's had for an hour,' the nurse sniggered.

Helen did not like to see patients as a source of amusement for the people who were supposed to be looking after them. She took her work and the well-being of patients extremely seriously, and if they could not receive the attention and care they deserved in a hospital, then where could they? Sometimes she wondered why some people ever chose nursing as a career.

It was a constant source of irritation to her. She had found the same at her previous hospital, and although generally, most nurses were dedicated and kind, a small minority didn't treat patients with the respect they deserved. Instead they saw them as an easy target for derision. Helen made no secret of the fact that it irritated the hell out of her.

A brisk walk along the corridor took Helen to the ward she would be responsible for - Ward Ten - and she located the sister's office. The door was ajar so she went in. To her dismay, she found that the cold as ice Sister Thornton was in charge of her ward – her patients.

The woman turned on her swivel-chair to face Helen. 'Good-morning Doctor Ross, can I help you? I daresay you wish to see some of your patients,' she said, sternly.

'Yes, that's right, and if I may, I'd like to make a start with Maria Dobson. Would that be okay?'

'You can see her of course, but she's currently sedated. You won't get any sense out of her. Still, if that's what you wish...'

'It is, yes.'

'She's in a side-ward; I'll take you to her. Follow me please.'

'Thank you, I appreciate it,' Helen said graciously.

She followed Sister Thornton the few yards from her office to where Maria Dobson lay prostrate and motionless in bed, her eyes firmly closed. The heavy curtains were drawn shut so that there was barely any light in the room. Helen approached the bedside, closely followed by the sister. Even in sleep the woman's face looked contorted in anguish. Helen took her ice-cold hand and held it. She turned to Sister Thornton who stood close behind her.

'How long has she been sedated for?'

'Around seventeen hours. Professor Kirkby felt it was the best thing for her, and I agree.'

'And how long was the professor planning to continue this sedation?'

'At least another day, I believe.'

'Well, I'd like to cease any further sedation for now. I want to see her awake.'

'I'm not sure the professor would approve of that,' the woman said.

'Well, it's not up to him any longer, is it? She's my patient now. So I'd appreciate it if you would see to it, alright?'

At that moment, Helen felt the patient's hand weakly squeezing hers. 'That'll be all for now, Sister, I'll let you get back to your work. I'm just going to stay with her for a moment.'

'What about your other patients? Don't you want to see them?'

Maria's hand began to squeeze harder.

'Yes, of course, I'll see them shortly, but I also hope to see them all over the next couple of days in my office, *not* on the ward.'

'I see. Well I'll leave you then.'

'Thank you,' Helen said. 'I'll see you in a minute or so.'

The woman reluctantly left the room, being sure to leave the door ajar as she did. Helen immediately closed it and returned to her patient, taking her hand once again, stroking the palm gently with her thumb. Slowly, Maria's eyes began to open until she eventually focused them on Helen.

'It's you – you came back, you promised you would,' she whispered. 'Please, you are going to help me, aren't you?'

Seven

'That's what I'm here for,' Helen said, gently squeezing her hand.

'I have to get out of here. Doctor Munroe was going to help me, she said she would, but then I never saw her again. She promised she would help me.'

'It's alright Maria, it's alright, try to keep calm now. I'm going to do everything I can to get you better.'

'Oh God, no, you're one of them, aren't you? You don't seem like one of them, but you are, aren't you?'

'Shh, everything's going to be alright,' she said, tucking a loose strand of hair behind Maria's ear.

'You don't understand; I'm not ill. I shouldn't be here.'

Helen sighed inwardly. Perhaps the professor was right in his diagnosis; maybe she *was* delusional and acutely paranoid – end of story. Yet there was something about the woman which cried out to her that something was not quite right, though exactly what at this stage she couldn't say.

'Look, as soon as you feel a little calmer, I'll take you along to my office where we can talk properly – how does that sound?'

The woman nodded eagerly. 'When?'

'Well, how about this afternoon? After you've had something to eat at lunchtime. Does that sound okay?' Helen said, pulling the curtains open.

Maria narrowed her eyes as the light flooded in. 'Yes, I

suppose so,' she said hoarsely. Helen poured out a glass of water and handed it to her as she sat more upright in the bed. She took a sip, also moistening her dry lips. 'How long have I been asleep? I lose track of time here,' she said with sadness in her voice.

'About a day, but don't worry about that, you needed rest. Look, I have to go now, Maria, but I promise I'll see you later, you have my word, okay?'

Maria forced a smile. 'Okay,' she said, and rolled over onto her side as Helen left.

'She's awake and seems calm enough now,' Helen said, as she returned to the sister's office. 'As I said, I'd like to keep her awake for now – no more sedation. I'm going to see her in my office after she's had some lunch. I'll take a look at the other patients now, if that's alright.'

'Of course,' the sister said sternly. 'I'll be along in a moment.'

Helen went ahead into the ward. She had twenty patients under her care, but not all were present. A couple of them had been pointed out to her in the day room earlier. All of her patients were female; some were curled up in bed, others sat on their beds, and a few wandered aimlessly, trance-like, about the ward, their heads rocking and arms jerking fitfully.

Sister Thornton followed quickly behind Helen. She bellowed an order for them all to get into their beds. 'Come along now, hurry up,' she added, and despite their obvious state of mind, with a little encouragement from the one and only nurse, they immediately and blindly obeyed.

As Helen saw each patient in turn, looked at their drug

charts, and attempted to speak with them, it became obvious that they were either far less alert, even than Maria, or they feared speaking in the presence of Sister Thornton. The woman stood looking over Helen's shoulder at all times. Helen could barely prise a word from any of them.

When she had visited each bedside, Helen turned to the sister. 'I'm clearly not going to be able to see all of them on a one-to-one basis today.' She paused thoughtfully. 'Actually, you know what? I think I'll just see Maria this afternoon and then five patients the next day and so on. I'll let you know who to send to me and when.' Sister Thornton simply nodded.

Helen couldn't help feeling the woman would be more suited to a career as a prison officer, she was harsh in looks as well as in her superior, gruff tone of voice. She was tall, at least six-feet, Helen guessed, and extremely hefty. What's more, it seemed to Helen the woman resented her for being young, being a qualified doctor, and not least, for having a strong character. On the other hand, maybe she was brusque with everyone – everyone, with the exception perhaps of Professor Kirkby.

Judging by her manner whilst in the company of Kirkby, the woman obviously held him in high esteem. Maybe there was something more going on between them than met the eye. Was it possible they were lovers? The woman dwarfed the professor in every physical way – the image that popped into her head of the two of them didn't bear thinking about. Helen laughed inwardly at her idle speculation.

'Alright Sister, if you could have a nursing assistant bring Maria to my office at 2.30, that would be great.'

'Very well,' the sister said curtly, as she returned to her desk. As she seated herself, she turned and spoke, stopping Helen in her tracks. 'By the way, Doctor Ross, if you want my opinion, you're making a mistake stopping the sedation of Maria Dobson. She's highly unstable.'

'Well, if you're correct, I'll soon find out, won't I? The decision can always be reversed, but for now, that is my decision. See you at lunch then.' Helen left her words hanging in the air as she left the sister's office and returned to her own.

∞∞∞∞

The day was an extremely grey one. The rain was steady and it had become so dark and overcast, it was necessary for Helen to flick on her desk lamp to make notes on the patients she had just seen. Although she had not mentioned it as a concern to the sister, she found that most of them displayed an abnormal degree of fear of her and Sister Thornton, who had hovered over Helen at all times during her preliminary examinations.

As always, she had tried to put each patient at as much ease as possible. However, nothing had worked with them; some of them had even cowered from her, covering their faces with their hands or shrinking away under the bed sheets. It had proved difficult, if not impossible, to reach any conclusions; she needed to see them in the confines of her office, well away from the ward and Sister Thornton.

Once back in her office, Helen took her patient files from the filing cabinet. She hesitated for a moment, wondering whether to go through the diary she had hidden there. She decided that she would read it in more detail later, perhaps in her room where she was certain not to be disturbed. She sat at her desk and started to make brief notes on each of the patients she had seen. All the notes were the same: *extreme anxiety displayed. Contributory factors inconclusive at this time.* And although there was no indication of paranoia on their records, she added: *possible paranoid tendencies.* The notes included those of Maria's.

She then added the patients in batches of five each day over the following few days in her diary. But this afternoon she would begin with Maria, when hopefully the effects of the sedation would have worn off enough for Helen to learn more about her problems. She glanced at her watch; there were still fifteen minutes until lunch. She poured herself a cup of coffee and, although it had been her intention to leave going through the hidden diary until the evening, temptation got the better of her.

Perhaps for the best, it wasn't to be, because as she stooped down and slid open the bottom drawer of the filing cabinet, her office door swung open and Kate stood in the doorway. Helen swiftly pushed the drawer closed again.

'Hi, how are things? Had a good morning?'

'Not bad, thanks,' replied Helen, standing up. 'How about you?'

'Oh, you know, pretty standard. Thought I was going to have kittens in the meeting this morning, but apart from that…'

'Why is everyone so scared of him, so scared to speak their minds?'

Kate shrugged and changed the subject. 'Anyway, you ready for lunch?'

'Yes, I suppose... mustn't be late now, must we?' Kate gave an embarrassed smile. 'Kate, I'm eating out this evening,' continued Helen, 'I'm going to the pub, it's only about six miles away – fancy joining me?'

'You're eating out? Does the professor know?'

'Yes, he knows, Helen said casually.'

'I – I don't know, I'll think about it. What on earth did he say?'

'What could he say? We work here, Kate, we're not patients – *or* prisoners. If you want to come with me, just come, you don't need permission.'

'Yes, well, as I said, I'll think about it, Helen.' She seemed uncomfortable and awkward. 'Look, we'd better go, it's almost 1 o'clock.'

Helen looked at her ponderingly for a moment and said with a cynical smile, 'okay, Kate.'

∞∞∞∞

Lunch came and went in virtual silence. Kirkby was by no means his usual hedonistic self, in fact he seemed somewhat subdued from the man Helen had got to know over the last two days. Was it only two days? To Helen, it seemed longer. She'd attempted to strike up a conversation with the other doctors, yet all seemed reticent to engage with her at any length, apart from Kirkby, who at one stage stated: 'I hear you're seeing Maria in your office this afternoon, Helen.

Well, good luck with that.' Sister Thornton had clearly briefed him. Mostly they just ate their lunch quietly, while the professor looked on sullenly, uncharacteristically picking at his food. Occasionally his eyes would meet disdainfully with Helen's. She could see their working relationship was going to be a bumpy one.

As Helen and Kate left the dining room, Helen reiterated her invitation regarding having dinner at the local pub. Kate was once again evasive, saying she would let her know later. Helen wasn't optimistic that the answer would be a yes. Still, she had tried. She didn't want to labour the point any more than necessary, nevertheless, Kate, and the others it seemed, required a really hard jolt.

They parted company at Helen's office and, as she entered, she shook her head in dismay at her new friend's timidity, fear, or whatever it might be that was holding her back from agreeing to go off site for a simple dinner. But for now, there were more important issues that required her attention – her patients.

She perused the notes for Maria Dobson once again. It appeared she had a long history of paranoid schizophrenia, as she had noticed the day before, had all her patients. Zyprexa and Seroquel had both been the main medication of choice by her predecessor and, according to the records, were still being administered. There was no doubt that these were probably the most effective drugs for controlling this condition, there was no good reason she could think of to change them, at least not for now.

After pouring herself a coffee, she picked up the phone, rang

Sister Thornton and asked for Maria to be brought to her office. The sister, being her usual charming self, told Helen she would send her as soon as a nursing assistant was available, adding defiantly that it might be some time.

'Wretched woman!' she said, replacing the handset. 'My God, what do you have to do around here to get some simple co-operation?' She took a deep, deep breath, tried to stay calm and waited for the arrival of her patient.

Around fifteen minutes elapsed before there was finally a knock on her door and a nursing assistant in her battle-grey top and white trousers pushed it open with the wheel-chaired Maria. After Helen assisted them in getting through the narrow door space, the assistant, an amiable young woman, left.

'Hello Maria, are you comfortable enough, or would you prefer to have an ordinary chair, or perhaps to lie down?'

She still appeared quite drowsy, a little confused, but nevertheless, reasonably composed. 'I think I'm alright here, thank you. Where's Doctor – Doctor...?'

'Doctor Munroe, you mean? She left the hospital. Do you remember seeing me yesterday and this morning, Maria?'

Maria looked blankly at her.

'Well, I'm Doctor Ross, but you can call me Helen, okay?'

'Doctor Munroe, yes, she was going to help me.'

'And I'm going to help you too, Maria. Would you like a glass of water?'

She shook her head and began to look agitated. 'You think I'm mad too, don't you? Well, I'm not fucking mad, at least I wasn't. No, they're the ones who are mad, not me; they're all trying to drive me fucking mad, you see. And you, you're probably one of *them* too, aren't you?'

Helen brought her chair close to Maria and held her hand. 'Try to stay calm now. I don't think you're mad, Maria, and I *am* going to help you, I promise. Now, who are *they*? And why do you think they are trying to drive you mad?'

'The bald-headed man and that sister. They do things to me you see, horrible things. Please help me,' she said, becoming more hysterical.

'Shh, you're quite safe with me. I'm not going to let anyone hurt you.'

'You can't protect me – not all the time, not at night. That's when they come, that's when they do things to me and the others.'

'So you don't think it's just you then?'

'They do it to everyone.'

Helen paused for a moment. 'Maria, do you know why you're here? In the hospital, I mean.'

She shook her head.

'Okay, and do you know how long you've been here?' Helen asked, consulting her notes.

'I'm not sure, a few months.'

'That's really what you think, just a few months?'

'I think so.'

Helen sighed. 'Maria, I'm sorry, but you've been here for just over a year.'

Eight

The session left Helen puzzled. She found it disconcerting that her patient had such little awareness of the time that had elapsed from first entering the institution. But there were other factors; like her being utterly convinced that she had not been ill before coming to The Manor. Yes, it was possible she was delusional as the professor had said, yet somehow, Helen didn't entirely believe that to be the case.

Helen had called the sister and asked that someone come to take Maria back to the ward. She had also sent a note ordering that her current medication be reduced and that she be given a daily dose of Mirtazapine and Olanzapine to control her anxiety.

Sister Thornton called Helen's office soon after and queried the order, but after some difference of opinion, reluctantly agreed to carry out her instructions. In any case, she had no choice in the matter, she could have argued about it, disagreed with the change in medication, but she knew that Helen's word was final.

At the end of her shift, Helen took the diary she had hidden, placed it in her briefcase and went to her room. She preferred that no one see it – or see her reading it, and at this point, though she had no reason to distrust her, that included Kate. She pondered about her first real days' work, about Maria, about the professor and his cronies. There was something about The Manor that gave her the creeps, something about the place that didn't feel right and something equally disturbing about its staff.

Helen turned on the shower, slipped out of her clothes, put on a bathrobe and switched on her coffee maker while she waited for hot water to appear from the rather grimy showerhead. She would take it off and give it a good clean when she had time. After several minutes when the water was hot enough, she hung up her robe and stepped in, arching her neck to allow the jet of steaming water to hit her face for a few moments.

As she massaged her body with a sponge loaded with soap, her cares and worries left her temporarily, although thoughts of Peter somehow managed to sneak into her mind. How was he coping? What was he doing right now? she wondered. Was he happy, or missing her? It was true she missed him and it would certainly be good to talk to him. But it couldn't be; she knew she had done the only decent thing she could have by ending their affair. Still, it would be nice to have someone in whom she could confide.

But then he wasn't here, she thought. He was miles away, working in a bright London hospital that saw an impressive recovery rate for patients. With his cold logic, he would almost certainly dismiss her apprehension as nothing but new job nerves and an overactive imagination, and who could say; perhaps he would be right. She had, after all, no evidence of any wrong-doing or mistreatment, only suspicions and the ramblings of a single patient.

There again, she thought, stepping out of the shower, there was the diary of her predecessor; that could not be put down to imagination. She hadn't even had the chance to read it all the way through, yet what she had read disturbed her greatly.

A few moments later her coffee was ready, and she took sips as she blew dry her hair. She cursed as a knock came at her door. 'Who is it?'

'It's me, Kate.'

A beaming smile greeted her as she opened the door. 'Hi, sorry to disturb you, I just wondered, is that invitation to dinner at the pub still open?'

Helen, a little shocked, said, 'yes, of course it is.'

'Oh great! Well in that case, I'd love to join you. What time?'

'Uh, well, I was thinking of leaving at around seven.'

'Okay, I'll go and get ready then. You're sure you don't mind me coming along?'

Helen, a little surprised, shook her head. 'No, not at all, but what about Professor Kirkby? Have you told him?'

'Yes.'

'And how was he about it?'

'Well, you know what he's like. Anyway, better let you go, you'll catch your death. I'll see you soon, then.'

'Look forward to it,' Helen said with a cheerful smile.

∞∞∞∞

It was raining steadily as they drove the few short miles to The Drunken Duck. Apart from a few private houses, it was the closest thing to civilisation in the whole area. The pub was a whitewashed stone building with a slate roof and a cosy glow emanated from its small windows as they pulled up in Helen's car outside.

Surprisingly, considering how sparsely populated the area was, there were several customers, a few diners whom she suspected were sightseers, and others standing around the bar, drinking real ale and chatting loudly amongst themselves.

'Yes ladies, what can I get you?' asked the friendly, round landlord.

'Good evening, could I have a glass of medium white wine please,' Helen said.

'Make that two,' Kate piped up. 'And could we order some food?'

'Of course, the menus are on the tables; just let me know what you want when you're ready. I can recommend my wife's home-made steak and kidney pie, it's quite famous around these parts,' he said with a smile.

'You've convinced *me*' – Helen said. What do you think, Kate?'

'Yes, I think I'll go for that, too.'

'You don't have to, choose whatever you like,' Helen said, 'we're not at The Manor now.'

'No, that'll be fine, honestly.'

'So, you both work at the hospital then, do you?' the landlord said, filling the glasses. 'You nurses, are you?'

'Doctors, actually. I've only just started there myself.'

'Really? Strange, we never seem to have anyone else from there come in for a drink or a meal, not for years anyway.'

'Hmm, yes, I can imagine,' Helen said, cynically glancing at Kate.

'Seems we have a pub full of doctors tonight then. See that gent at the end of the bar? He's our resident quack. Well, he's not a quack; he's very good actually. Would you like me to introduce you to him? Seeing as you're both sort of in the same profession, so to speak.'

It was tempting. He was in his thirties, Helen guessed, and ruggedly good-looking, and perhaps if she had been there alone she would have taken up the landlord's offer. She already craved the company of someone normal.

'That's very kind of you,' she said, 'but maybe another time.'

They took a table in a corner, slipped off their coats and sat down facing one another.

'So, you've never been here before?' Helen asked. 'Are you seriously telling me you've never been off the hospital premises in all the time you've been there?'

'Yes, pretty much.'

'I'm sorry Kate; I just can't get my head round it – why? I mean, not just you, but all the others. Why do you all let Kirkby rule you so much? You must see it's not normal.'

'It's nice here, isn't it,' Kate said, looking around the bar with a smile - the smile of a child experiencing something magical for the first time. 'I know I've said things about him, but he's a good man really,' she added, 'he has ours and the patients best interests at heart.'

'Your best interests? You're joking, right?'

'No,' she said, looking more serious, 'he really has.'

'I see.' It seemed to Helen that her colleague had changed in a matter of hours, either out of blind loyalty to Kirkby, or perhaps she was in fear of him. 'How well did you know Doctor Munroe?'

'Doctor Munroe? Not very well, she didn't fit in too well.'

'Oh, in what way?'

'Oh, I don't know, she just kept herself to herself. Not at all like you, Helen.'

'Is that why she left – because she didn't fit in?'

Kate shrugged. 'I suppose so, I don't really know.'

'I'm sorry, Kate, it must seem like I'm asking an awful lot of questions. Let's not talk about work anymore tonight.' She picked up her glass and held it in the air. 'Cheers!' she said, before taking a much needed sip.

Their meal arrived shortly afterwards, served by a jolly woman whom Helen presumed was the landlord's wife, and the cook. They ate in silence, occasionally perusing the people in the bar. Helen was famished and finished quickly, then placing her knife and fork on her empty plate, she turned to Kate.

'Actually, you know what? I think I'm going to have another one of these,' she said, lifting her glass. 'How about you, would you like another?'

'No, not for me, I'm fine thanks.'

Helen made her way to the bar and as the landlord slowly poured a pint for one of the locals, her eyes briefly met with those of the doctor who was standing at the opposite end of the bar. He was now in what appeared deep and serious conversation with another man, yet his attention veered and his and Helen's eyes met once again. She thought for a moment he even smiled.

'What can I get you, same again my love?' asked the landlord, interrupting her thoughts.

'Just another white wine, please.'

With his back to Helen, the landlord poured out the wine into a clean glass. 'So, you're new up there at The Manor you say?'

'Yes, that's right, started yesterday.'

'Hmm,' he drew closer and almost whispered, 'I hope you don't mind me saying, but there's something strange about that place. Everyone around here thinks so, I think even young Doctor Hamilton over there thinks so, although he won't admit as much. You should speak to him when you're next in. You will be in again, I hope?'

'Yes, I'm sure I will. Strange? In what way?'

'Best not to talk now. Just be careful, that's all I'll say.'

Helen laughed. 'Sounds rather dramatic, but yes, thank you, I will,' she said.

The man's references to the hospital seemed odd to say the least, but she supposed it was probably nothing more than local gossip and prejudice towards a mental institution. The Manor also took on a sinister appearance in its isolated spot on the moors and tales were often abound about old buildings and what went on inside them.

Helen returned to the table where Kate was still picking at her meal. 'What's wrong, not hungry?'

'Not terribly, no – sorry.'

'Don't apologise, but you should try to eat something.'

Kate flicked her eyes towards the bar. 'What was the man talking to you about?'

'Oh, nothing much, you know, just small-talk.' She took a sip of her drink. 'Is something wrong? You seem a little on edge.'

'No, everything's fine.'

Helen studied her for a moment. 'It probably just feels a little strange – being out I mean.'

'Yes, I suppose it does a bit.'

'Well, we should make a point of doing it at least once a week, don't you think?'

'Yes,' she said. 'That would be nice.'

'So, are you from around here, Kate?'

'No, I'm originally from London.'

'I thought your accent wasn't local. What brought you to work at The Manor?'

'Oh, I don't know, it just seemed like a good idea at the time.' She hesitated to go further, but eventually continued. 'Well, as a matter of fact, I came here to get away from someone. As I said, it seemed like a good idea at the time. That must sound strange.'

Helen smiled. 'No, on the contrary, I can relate to that perfectly well – I take it we're talking about a man?'

'Yes.'

'In that case, between you and me, we have something very much in common.'

'Really?'

'Yes, really.'

'But you seem so strong, Helen. I can't imagine you running away from *anything*.'

'Well I did, believe me. The only trouble is, now I'm

beginning to wonder if I did the right thing in leaving London.'

'Well, you're here now. I'm sure you did do the right thing. I really hope you stay, Helen.'

'As you rightly say, I'm here now, for better or worse. I have to say though, I do find the place a bit odd, or perhaps I should say – the people.'

'Does that include me? I probably do come across as a bit of an oddball to you.'

'No, of course not, but you must see yourself that the others are a little strange, surely? Not least, Kirkby.'

'He's eccentric, a little quirky, I grant you.'

'Quirky Kirkby!' Helen said, sniggering. 'Joking aside,' she continued after a long pause, 'you're afraid of him, aren't you?'

'Maybe, maybe just a little. But not so much as the place itself. It has history, you see.'

'These former asylums usually do – and it's usually all myth, local folklore and legends. The place can't harm you, but being treated badly by Kirkby *can*. I think he's messed with yours and the others minds by making you feel like prisoners, and that's not on, Kate. Anyway, I won't nag you anymore, you've made a start by being here tonight. Let's just enjoy the evening and not talk about work anymore, shall we?'

'Fair enough, that suits me. But you're wrong, Helen. It's not as you say, myths and legends. The place is evil. I know; I've seen it with my own eyes.'

Nine

Throughout the remainder of the evening, the atmosphere had become subdued. Not that she believed in that sort of thing, but Helen couldn't resist pushing Kate a little further to tell her more about her experiences at the hospital. She didn't wish to talk about it though; it was as if she were exhausted by opening up as much as she had. They drove back to The Manor in silence; a low-lying layer of mist covered the open moorland and a steady rain made the short journey seem all the more melancholy.

Soon the imposing building came into view, emerging from the moors and the mist like a solitary colossus. The two parted company, each going to their respective living quarters, and each bidding one another goodnight in a sombre mood. It was only just after nine, and yet the darkness of the corridor made it feel much later.

Helen hung up her coat, flicked off her shoes, and made some coffee before lying on the bed and plugging in the earphones to her iPhone. She selected a playlist, Mozart, she always found it relaxing, then lay back, pondering all that Kate had said to her in the pub. It was apparent to Helen that her new colleague had issues: mood swings, nervousness, perhaps an overactive imagination, which was, Helen thought, most likely brought about by isolation from the outside world, not by any evil presence.

The notion puzzled Helen. That a young woman of science

could believe a place was evil rather than analyse the situation to reach the logical conclusion that her anxieties were caused by nothing more than remoteness and loneliness. Kate had said she'd been working at the hospital for a year. If in all that time she had not been out to socialise, to meet other people, then it was little wonder she was feeling the strain. And if it were the case that the other members of staff never ventured outside the confines of the hospital, it would also explain why they, too, acted so strangely and in most cases were so insular.

The Mozart wasn't working on this occasion and she found herself feeling restless. She stretched, still with her earphones plugged in, for her briefcase at the side of her bed and pulled out the diary. She intended to read it through in more detail, yet once again she felt restless and distracted by her thoughts and placed it next to her on the bed.

With realisation as to the cause of her unwanted restlessness, she took out her earphones, pressed pause, and opened her contacts, scrolling down until she landed on Peter's number. Her finger hovered over it for a moment. She missed him, but more than that perhaps, she needed contact with the outside world; it seemed an eternity since she had spoken to anyone other than the staff of The Manor.

Helen agonised for a moment, her finger still poised. Would it be right to phone him? It had been her that had brought the relationship to an end, would it be fair to him, his wife, or to her to make contact? She desperately wanted to hear his voice, but no, she thought; it wouldn't be right. She even felt herself getting a little angry at the fact he hadn't considered contacting *her*, if for no other reason, simply to check that she was okay. After all, he had no idea where she had gone. Had he got over their affair so easily that he no longer cared?

There was, however, another reason for making contact with the outside world, not simply to hear the voice of someone normal, but to find out anything she could about the author of the diary, Doctor Munroe, and her present whereabouts. Of course, there was little you couldn't find out on the web, and if it came to it, that was what she would do. But such was her desire to speak to someone, she scrolled up her list of contacts until she found the number of a good friend and colleague at her old hospital.

She hesitated before tapping the call button. How could she explain her interest without sounding mysterious? It was too late though, her fingertip had made a feather light connection with the call button icon and the number was already dialling.

After around three rings, the call was answered.

'Hi Mel, its Helen. Are you at work?'

'Helen! It's so good to hear from you! No, I'm off duty tonight. How are you? How's the new job going?'

Helen sank back against the pillows. 'Well, it's different, shall we say. How are things with you?'

'Fine, overworked and underpaid as always, but apart from that, pretty good. So, tell me all, what's it like there?'

'Well, the staff are a bit odd to say the least. I only hope I did the right thing coming here.'

'It always feels strange when you start a new job, I'm sure you'll be fine once you've settled in, though I do miss you. Not quite the same without you.'

'I miss you too,' she said, her eyes wandering around the

sparsely decorated room, 'and the hospital.'

'And Peter?'

'Well…'

'I'm sorry, I shouldn't have…'

'That's okay, Mel. I don't regret finishing it. It was the only decent thing I could do. Actually, I was wondering if you could do me a favour.'

'Yes, of course. What is it?'

She paused for a moment, forming the words in her head. The last thing she wanted was for Mel to think she was being irrational. 'I was wondering if you could ask around about my new boss, Professor John Kirkby, and also Doctor Elise Munroe, you know, see what you can find out about them. I'm particularly interested to know where Doctor Munroe went from here – I'm her replacement, you see.'

Mel scribbled down the names as Helen spoke. 'Yes, sure, I'll see what I can do. This all sounds very mysterious, Helen, what's going on?'

'Oh, nothing really, just curious. If I'm honest, Mel, I could probably find out a little by myself by trolling the web. The truth is, I've only been here two days and I'm finding it a bit lonely. It's just good to hear a friendly voice.'

'Yes, well, I must admit, when you told me where you were going, I thought it was rather a big step just to avoid contact with Peter. You could always come back – you're missed, you know.'

'That's sweet of you, but I think I have to at least give it a chance, don't you?'

'I suppose so. Look, I'm on duty tomorrow, I'll see what I

can dig up and give you a call tomorrow evening. Would that be okay?'

'Yes, that'd be marvellous, thanks, Mel.'

'Okay, take care and I'll speak to you tomorrow – bye for now, Helen, byee.'

It was good to hear her friend's voice, but now there was silence and solitude once again. "You could always come back," Mel had said. It was tempting. But how would it look? She could imagine the management's view of her as she asked for her old job back. It wouldn't impress them much, and who could blame them? If she were in their shoes, she would feel exactly the same.

It was all idle speculation in any case; she would not return with her tail between her legs, begging to be taken back after only days. Even if it were weeks or months, she had her pride and it would be completely unthinkable. Not only that, but it seemed there were patients at The Manor who seriously needed help and she wasn't about to abandon them; she would never be able to live with herself if she did. So this was it, for now at least. She was committed to staying put and caring for her patients, no matter what.

∞∞∞∞

Helen was in pyjamas and in bed, reading through the diary of Elise Munroe. It was around midnight when she heard the faint sound of footsteps outside her door and picking up pace along the corridor. The footsteps, if that was what she'd heard, sounded furtive, yet at the same time, urgent. What's more, it seemed as if they had originated from Kate's room.

 Like herself, Kate was on call at night. Perhaps there was some kind of crisis on her ward that required her attention, though she had heard no phone ringing, nor any pager, which she was certain she would have heard. She placed the diary on her bedside table, slithered out of bed and put on a heavy dressing gown; the room was as cold as ice.

 She rushed to her door, opened it and peered out into the gloomy corridor. As they were the only two occupying the wing she could only assume it to be Kate, but whoever it was had quickly disappeared. Helen was curious but couldn't interfere; it was clearly none of her concern. Nevertheless, she found herself slipping into a pair of trousers, a tee-shirt, donning her white coat and heading out of her room.

 Quite what her intention was, she had no idea. She was restless in any case and however odd it may have seemed, no one could question her taking a midnight stroll or even taking the opportunity of making an impromptu visit to her ward. That said, it seemed to Helen that nothing was so straightforward at this particular hospital.

 She made her way swiftly along the dark corridor. The place had an atmosphere that made her shudder, a sense of loneliness and hopelessness crept along its very walls making her uneasy and inexplicably anxious.

 It was with relief that she emerged from the corridor into the reception area, though it was only partially lit now. The main source of light emanated from the receptionist's hatch and spread across the floor. The deathly silence had only been broken by the momentary buzzing sound of the electronic door catch being released as Helen entered the area.

A voice came from the office. 'Who's that?' Helen instantly recognised the sharp, cold voice as that of Mary's. She emerged from her office and into the reception hall before Helen could respond.

'Oh, it's you. Can I help you?' she said indignantly. Helen loathed the woman and her disrespectful manner. Was it simply that the woman had taken a dislike to her, or was she this rude to everyone? Helen wondered.

'No, I'm visiting my ward – is that okay with you?' Helen said sarcastically.

'At this time of night? I hope you don't wake them all up.'

'Have I done something to offend you?' Helen said, glaring at her. 'Look, Mary, let me make myself clear – what I do with my patients is my concern, not yours. Do you understand?'

The woman was taken aback and for once was speechless.

'Now, I suggest you get back to your work and let me carry on with mine,' Helen continued. She didn't wait for a response, but instead proceeded straight to the door which led to the wards and tapped in the security key. The door buzzed, opened, and Helen went through, simply glancing over her shoulder at the shocked Mary.

Helen smiled to herself as she walked along the corridor. She suspected the awful woman had never received such a rebuke before and it felt really quite good. Perhaps, just perhaps, next time the woman would think twice about being so rude and disrespectful.

She approached Ward Eleven; it was the ward which Kate

was in charge of. There seemed to be no sign of anything happening as she peered through the glass window of the door, which then led along another short corridor into the ward itself. There was only a hint of light, which came from the night lights in the ward at the end of the passageway. There was no movement, no sign of Kate, nothing. All seemed well. So where was Kate?

She felt vulnerable peering through the door; it would look very strange should someone come along. She looked around to satisfy herself she was not being seen. It was stupid, she didn't know what she expected to find anyway, and entering a ward that she had no official right to be in would be impossible to explain. How could she justify her snooping to the duty nurse? No! It was out of the question.

However, her ward, the next ward along, was a different matter; she had every right to pay a visit whenever she wished, so she decided that while she was up and now wide awake, she may as well do just that. She walked the few yards to Ward Ten, pushed open the swing doors and confidently made her way to the office.

The duty nurse, a staff nurse she had not met before, was sat at her desk writing notes. The suddenness of Helen's voice saying, 'good-morning' caused her to physically jump and instinctively swivel round in her chair. The woman, in her thirties, held her heart for a moment before regaining composure.

'Sorry, I shouldn't have crept up on you like that,' Helen said apologetically. 'We haven't met, I'm…'

'Doctor Ross, isn't it? That's okay, Staff Nurse Cooper,

pleased to meet you, Doctor. I'm sorry about that; it's just that you can get a bit spooked in this place at night sometimes. Is there something wrong? Only we don't usually get night visits from doctors.'

'No, nothing wrong. To tell you the truth I couldn't sleep. Anything happening? All the patients tucked up?'

'Yes, all very quiet, nothing going on at all.'

'That's good. Mind if I take a look around quietly?'

'No, of course not, Doctor, it's your ward. Would you like me to come with you?'

'Yes, please do, that is if you're not too busy with paperwork.'

'Oh no,' she said, getting to her feet. 'I'll have all night to do that hopefully, barring any incidents or disturbances.'

As they walked, Helen asked in a hushed voice, 'do you have many disturbances?'

'Not usually, no, but occasionally, as you'd expect, there are problems, you know, minor episodes, that sort of thing.'

'Yes, of course, that's only to be expected, isn't it? How did you get on with Doctor Munroe, by the way?' Helen asked, as they walked slowly and quietly past each patient's bed.

'I always got on very well with her. She left very suddenly, never even had a chance to say goodbye. Quite strange really.'

'Any idea where she went after here?'

'No, none at all.' She paused before continuing. 'Can I speak frankly with you, Doctor?'

'Yes, you can, absolutely.'

The nurse looked at Helen warily. 'I don't know if I should, I don't want to lose my job – I can't afford to, but...'

'Look.' Helen reached out and held the woman's arm. 'I promise whatever you say to me will be in the strictest confidence – it'll go no further, you have my word. It'll be between you and me – no one else.'

There was another look of caution from the nurse. 'I wasn't entirely honest a moment ago when I said there were only a few disturbances during the nights here. Truth is, they're quite frequent. I'm not sure what's going on, but every now and then Professor Kirkby or Sister Thornton comes to the ward and takes one of the patients away – sometimes for hours on end. It's been bothering me for ages and I didn't know what to do, but you seem like someone I can trust. I hope you are.'

'I promise, you *can* trust me,' said Helen reassuringly, 'I'll let you into a little secret. I've only been here two days and I'm already beginning to think there's something a little strange going on here myself.'

'You do?'

'Yes, I do, and I want to get to the bottom of it. What's your name by the way? I'm Helen.'

'Jenny.'

'Well, it's very good to meet you, Jenny. I think you're probably the first totally normal person I've met here so far. Tell me; is there a set pattern to these visits in the night by the professor?'

'No, not really, they seem to be completely at random, although it's always around midnight or sometimes later.'

'And he gives no warning or explanation?'

'No, never.'

'Do you keep records of the patients being removed from the ward?'

'No, the professor expressly tells me there's no need.'

Helen sighed, laying to rest her initial thoughts that she was just being irrational.' Look Jenny,' she said, 'keep this conversation to yourself, okay? I'm going to look into it, but don't worry, I'll do it discreetly, your name will never come up.'

They reached the bed of Maria Dobson. 'How's she doing?'

asked Helen, quietly.

'Not all that well. She's been having a lot of episodes recently and they're getting worse. She's peaceful enough now, of course, but that's because she's on the same night time sedation as all the others. Do you have a particular interest in her, Doctor?'

'You could say that.'

'I only ask because Maria's one of the patients the professor chooses to take away from the ward at night sometimes.'

'Is that so? Well that's *very* interesting.'

'What do you think's going on then?'

'I don't know, Jenny, perhaps nothing. I really don't know. Look, do you have a night off any time soon?'

'Yes, tomorrow as a matter of fact. Why?'

'Good. Do you fancy meeting me at The Drunken Duck for a drink?'

'Yes, that'd be nice.'

'If I'm going to get to the bottom of whatever is going on, I'll need help. Are you prepared for that?'

Jenny nodded, though her face was full of apprehension. 'I admit I'm a little scared, but yes, I'll help if I can.'

'That's settled then. 8 o'clock okay for you?'

'That's fine.'

'Okay, I'll see you there then,' Helen said as they reached the office. 'What do you make of Doctor Scott by the way?' she asked, turning to the nurse once again.

'Well, as she's in charge of Ward Eleven, I don't really see that much of her, but she seems okay. A little reserved maybe. Why? You don't think she's involved in... well, whatever's going on, if there *is* something going on.'

'No, I'm sure she isn't. I'll see you tomorrow, or maybe I should say, later today – goodnight Jenny.'

'Goodnight, Doctor.'

Helen left the ward and made her way along the corridor, stopping briefly to look through the windowed door of Ward Eleven once more. And once more, all seemed quiet – perhaps too quiet. Was Kate somehow involved in this late night spiriting away of patients? In all her time in the profession she had never heard of anything similar.

What possible purpose could there be for such actions? She could see no way how it would be beneficial for the unfortunate souls being taken from their beds, the one place where they might feel some relief from their torment, in the middle of the night. It seemed unthinkable that Kirkby would find it necessary to carry out treatments at such an hour – it made no sense and in her opinion was tantamount to cruelty.

What *was* good though, was that she now had someone she could trust, and she looked forward to their meeting later that day. By now it was 1am and time, she thought, for her late night wandering to end and to get some much needed sleep.

She left the corridor and entered the reception again. Suddenly she felt quite drained as she tapped in the security code on the door that led back to her living quarters. As she did so, knowing very well she would be listening, she called out with a hint of sarcasm, 'goodnight Mary.' She didn't wait for a response, but simply made her way as quickly as possible back to her room.

As she unlocked her door and entered her room, she

wondered if Kate had returned during her absence. The diary of Elise Munroe lay open on her bed, as she had left it. She would read no more tonight, she had the beginning of a headache, perhaps caused by the wine earlier, or through the strain she was already beginning to feel in her new job.

She undressed down to her tee shirt and pants and slipped into bed, not bothering with her pyjamas, and pulled the bed cover over her, falling asleep almost immediately. It was not a restful sleep that Helen found, but a sleep filled with dreams and portents, so that when she woke some six hours later, she felt unrested, uneasy and a little jittery.

At least breakfast was optional. Kirkby took his breakfast in his private apartment on the upper floor, but a buffet style breakfast was laid on in the dining room for any other senior staff who wished to partake. Helen decided that all she needed at the moment was her coffee and some painkillers for the headache, of which she was now becoming aware.

She managed to see a couple of her patients before proceeding to the mid-morning meeting in Kirkby's office. On her way she met Doctor Brownlow. He had raced to catch up with her in the corridor.

Alan Brownlow was reasonably good looking with light brown hair and pleasant enough in manner. 'Good morning,' he said, a little breathlessly.

'Good morning, Doctor,' Helen said, continuing to walk.

'What happened to you last night?'

She stopped in her tracks. 'What do you mean?'

'Dinner! The old man was in a foul mood all evening.'

'Oh, oh I see. I went out for dinner,' she said casually.

'You went out? No wonder he was in such a mood. We missed your company, well I certainly did anyway, but nobody dare bring up as to why you weren't there.'

'Maybe you should try it yourself some time.'

He turned away. 'Yes, well…'

'I mean it. I can't understand why everyone seems so scared of him.'

'Well, I wouldn't say we're scared of him exactly, it's just…'

'Yes?'

'Oh, nothing really, it's just that he can be very persuasive.'

'Look, I know I'm the new kid on the block, but if you ask me, he sees himself as some sort of demigod or something. The more you and the others indulge him, the worse he'll become. Do you know what I'm saying?'

'Yes, I…'

'Just don't let him push you around, that's all I'm saying.'

The man nodded. 'Yes, you're quite right of course.'

'Well, in that case, why don't you join me for dinner one evening at the pub down the road?' Helen immediately realised how it must have sounded, she had no interest in him in that way, but perhaps she was in some way attracted by his innocent charm.

He hesitated as they stopped outside Kirkby's office. 'Yes, why not,' he said eventually, 'that would be very nice.'

Helen smiled. 'How about tomorrow then?'

'Yes, alright, tomorrow it is.'

She felt the need to qualify her seeming forwardness as their eyes met. 'Strictly as colleagues, of course.'

'Of course.'

'Oh well, I suppose we'd better go in.'

As the previous day, the meeting went without any real issues being brought to the fore. Helen certainly had some, but for now kept them to herself. Professor Kirkby seemed lighter of mood with an almost permanent smile on his face. That was until the meeting concluded and the staff began to leave his office. He called out to Helen as she reached the door.

'I take it we'll have the pleasure of your company at dinner this evening, Doctor Ross?'

She turned to him. 'No, I'm afraid not, Professor, I'm dining out again, and possibly again tomorrow,' she said, glancing at Doctor Brownlow. His eyes darted nervously but avoided contact with hers. Helen wondered if, at the end of the day, he would have the courage to see it through. His silence somehow said everything.

Kirkby's smile disappeared immediately, though he said nothing. He simply adjusted his glasses, as it seemed he always did when flummoxed, picked up his pen with a despairing lament and flicked through some papers on his desk.

'Sorry about that,' Doctor Brownlow said, as they left the office, 'I'll have a word with him later.'

'There's no need to explain, Doctor,' Helen said indifferently. 'See you later.'

They parted company and Helen rushed to catch up with Kate. She, like Helen, was en-route to her office and had not, as she had before, hung back to wait for Helen. She hadn't even knocked on Helen's door earlier that morning so they could walk to their respective offices together.

'Morning, Kate,' Helen said.

'Oh, morning, Helen.' She seemed distracted, edgy and uncomfortable, and her complexion was even more pale than usual.

'You okay?'

'Yes, I'm fine.'

You don't look fine, if you don't mind me saying. Bad night?'

'No, just a slight headache, that's all.'

'Oh dear, maybe it was the wine I plied you with.'

'Yes, that's probably it.'

'Hmm,' Helen said, studying her.

'Oh, I'm not blaming you. I'm just not used to it, that's all.'

'Well, we should do it again, and maybe next time we should stick to soft drinks, eh?'

'Yes, that would be nice. Well, this is me,' Kate said, stopping at her office door. 'See you at lunch, Helen.'

'Yes okay, hope you feel better.'

Headache or no headache, Kate seemed far less approachable with Helen today. But then, she had seemed a little distant the previous evening as well. It was also very obvious she was hiding the fact she had left her room in the middle of the night. But why conceal it? What was she hiding?

The next question that entered Helen's head was simply, was Kate hiding anything at all? Perhaps there was nothing untoward going on at the hospital; perhaps it was nothing more than her imagination running wild. Yet somehow she knew that was not the case, she was not prone to flights of fancy, she was sure something was amiss. It was simply a matter of finding out what.

At the same time, although Kate was a slightly odd character, cheerful one moment, withdrawn the next, it was difficult to imagine her being part of anything remotely sinister. For a moment she considered poking her head round Kate's office door and asking if she would like to join Jenny Cooper and herself for drinks at the pub later, however, she thought better of it and continued on her way.

The day passed quietly. Helen had sessions of talking therapy with the next group of patients on her list. As before, she saw them individually. Some were difficult to communicate with, they were agitated and restless; a few were calmer, able to listen to and talk to Helen with relative composure.

It was a pleasant and an unexpected surprise that not all her patients were in quite such a poor mental state. In fact, a couple made her wonder why they were in such an institution in the first place and not receiving help and support from other resources. She decided, however, to monitor them before making any decision regarding discharging them. Besides, there was another matter to consider. As she had noted before, none of her patients had any next of kin, which in itself struck her as very peculiar.

Lunch was also a quiet, almost morose affair. Professor Kirkby had hardly spoken, except for a few exchanges with Sister Thornton and Doctor Wright and, to a lesser extent, the other doctors around the table. It seemed he deliberately excluded Helen; there was even an absence of his usual sarcastic remarks to contend with.

Doctor Brownlow, although seated almost exactly opposite Helen, managed to avoid any eye contact with her. It sent a very clear signal that he hadn't, and probably had no intention of broaching the subject with Kirkby regarding dinner the next evening. It seemed inconceivable that a grown man could be so afraid about such a matter. What made it worse was that he had no need to ask permission to go off the premises in the first place. How was it possible, she wondered, for Kirkby to have such power over these people?

∞∞∞

As she lay, propped up against the pillows on her bed, Helen watched the rain pelting against her window. It was 5.30pm and already dark as night. She finished her coffee and lay down to rest for an hour or so before leaving for the pub, and heard the door to Kate's room being pulled shut, the sound reverberating along the corridor. After setting her alarm she closed her eyes, hoping for sleep, but with her mind spinning so much, it wouldn't come.

Would Mel call her back tonight? she wondered. And if so, what, if anything, would she have found out about Kirkby and Elise Munroe? Thoughts of Peter also ran through her mind. Although she had no regrets about ending the relationship, mainly out of a sense of decency and concern for his wife, why hadn't he called her mobile to check that she was okay? It seemed so out of character somehow.

She had no doubt that Mel would call her back as soon as she could, but in the meantime she thought she would carry out some of her own research. She took her laptop, opened the web browser and first typed, Doctor Elise Munroe into the search box. There were several entries. She checked each one meticulously, they ranged from doctors of medicine to astronomers and all other manner of scientific disciplines, yet none of the listings were for doctors of psychiatry. It was as if she never existed.

Eleven

Helen made a dash from her car into The Drunken Duck; it was still raining heavily. Surprisingly, on such a night, the place was heaving, it was surprising in any case, as the pub was several miles from the nearest village, along a lonely winding road which cut through the moors. She assumed that would be where Jenny lived.

She was a little earlier than the time they had arranged to meet; she only hoped the nurse would not have a change of heart and decide not to show up.

'Hello there, my love, back again so soon?' said the landlord, as she jostled her way to one of the few available spaces at the bar. 'It's nice to see you again. What can I get you, white wine, wasn't it?'

'Thank you, that'd be lovely. You're very busy.'

'There's a darts match about to start. Not that I'm complaining. Will you be eating with us again tonight?'

'I'm not sure, maybe. I'm waiting for a friend to turn up, I'll let you know.'

'No rush, my love. In any case, if you only feel like a snack, there'll be sandwiches on offer later for the darts teams, we always make too many.'

'Thank you, that's very kind of you.'

At that moment, her mobile rang its discreet tone. She quickly handed the landlord a five pound note and rummaged through her handbag to locate the phone.

'Excuse me a moment,' she said, as she answered the call. 'Hi, Mel, how are you? she said, moving away from the crowded bar.

'Hi, Helen, sorry it's taken so long to get back to you. Where are you? It sounds quite rowdy.'

'In the local pub, anything to get away for a few hours. So, did you find anything?'

'Not a lot, I'm afraid. I couldn't find out anything about this Doctor Munroe you asked about. Professor Kirkby, on the other hand, I did manage to dig up something.'

'Sounds interesting.'

'Well, I'm not sure how interesting it really is. There's very little information on him except that up until a few years ago he worked at Porton Down, the government military science park.'

'*The* Porton Down? In Wiltshire?'

'Yes, the very same. That's all I have, I'm afraid. What he was involved in I have no idea, as you'd expect, there are no records.'

'What would a Professor of Psychiatry be doing working there?' she said.

'Good question. I have no idea, Helen. All I know is I wish you'd leave. I don't like the sound of that place.'

'I'll be fine, don't worry about me, I can look after myself.' Helen, looking towards the door, saw Jenny entering the pub. 'Look, I have to go, I'll give you a call tomorrow evening. And Mel – thanks.'

Helen waved to catch Jenny's attention as she looked

anxiously around the crowded bar. Their eyes met and both betrayed a smile of relief that each had actually turned up as agreed.

'Hi,' Helen said, 'glad you made it!'

After ordering Jenny a cranberry juice, they headed for the quiet table that Helen and Kate had sat at the night before; it was away from the crowded far end of the bar where the darts match was now well underway. They chatted briefly about what had prompted Helen to leave London, and of Jenny's life in the village, and then eventually their conversation turned to the matter in hand, the hospital.

'So,' Helen asked, 'did anything unusual happen last night – that is apart from *my* unexpected visit?

'No, nothing last night. It was very quiet.'

'Well, that's something anyway. Tell me more about Doctor Munroe, what was she like?'

'She was a very kind lady, very good with the patients. She really cared. That's why it was such a shock when she just upped and left the way she did. It was so unlike her, if you know what I mean.'

'Would it surprise you if I told you there seems to be no trace of her?'

Jenny looked at her curiously. 'What do you mean?'

'Just that! It's as if she never existed. Do you happen to know if she had any family?'

'I can't say for sure, but I imagine not. Like all the other doctors, she never seemed to leave the hospital for anything.'

'What about the time before she left, did you happen to notice any change in her?'

Jenny thought for a moment, idly circling the rim of her glass with her finger. 'Well, now that you mention it, yes, she seemed... I don't know, a little sad I suppose, a little more on edge as well.'

'The thing is, I found a...'

'Good evening ladies.' Helen instantly recognised the man standing over them as the local general practitioner the landlord had pointed out the previous evening.

'Good evening,' Helen replied, his disarming smile having no effect. In fact she was a little annoyed at the intrusion.

'Jim tells me you work at The Manor. I'm Stephen Hamilton; I'm a GP at the local practice.'

'Helen Ross,' she said, offering her hand, 'and this is Jenny Cooper.'

'Yes, I recognise *you* from the village,' he said to Jenny. 'Now, can I buy you two ladies a drink?'

Helen shook her head. 'That's very kind, but...'

'No buts, I insist, and then I promise I won't intrude on you any further. You're obviously in *deep* conversation.'

'If you absolutely insist, a glass of medium white and...'

'Cranberry juice please,' said Jenny.

'I'll be right back,' he said, grinning like a Cheshire cat.

'He's full of himself,' Helen said, as he headed to the bar. 'Is he actually your GP?'

'Yes, I believe so. I haven't been to the doctor for years. I've seen him around, though. Quite dishy, isn't he?'

'Oh, he's good looking enough,' Helen smiled, 'but boy, does he know it.'

Within moments he returned with their drinks, placed them

down on the table and pulled up a chair to join them. There was an awkward silence for a few moments until he spoke again. 'So, Helen, tell me all about yourself.'

'Nothing interesting to tell, I'm afraid,' she said. 'Look, I appreciate the drink, and I don't wish to be rude, but my friend and I were…'

'I'm sorry, yes, you're quite right.' He stood up. 'After all, I did promise not to disturb you. Well, maybe another time?'

'Yes, another time. I'm sorry, you must think I'm terrible, but…'

'Not at all, I understand. Well, goodnight ladies,' he said, the broad smile dissipating as he returned to his group.

'I feel awful now. Was I horribly rude?'

'You *were* pretty blunt,' Jenny said, cringing a little.

'Oh well, never mind. I was about to tell you, and please don't mention this to anyone. I found a diary of Doctor Munroe's, hidden at the back of her desk. It makes very interesting reading. I got the distinct impression she had discovered something about what's going on at The Manor and was about to blow the whistle.'

'What do you think she discovered exactly?'

'Well, that's where it's all a bit vague. But something is going on, I'm sure of it, and I aim to find out what. Can I rely on your help, Jenny?'

Jenny hesitated before answering. 'I'm sure you're right, something isn't right there, but I'll be honest, I'm scared.'

'I understand completely.'

'But yes, you can rely on me, Helen, I'll help. What do you want me to do?'

∞∞∞∞

The evening had been a pleasant one. They had not spent it entirely discussing the hospital; they had got to know one another better and by the time they left the pub, the two were firm friends. They had a great deal in common it seemed. Jenny, at thirty-two, like Helen, lived alone and had always done so since the death of her parents. She'd only had a couple of brief encounters with men since then; working permanent nights at the hospital made it impossible to form any kind of lasting relationship.

They spoke of men, their musical tastes, Helen feeling more at ease than she had since arriving at the Manor, even opening up about her affair with Peter.

But what was more important, they now had a plan.

'All I need from you,' said Helen, 'is that you call me on my mobile at any time of the night when a patient is removed and taken away. Can you do that? The rest will be up to me.'

'Yes, I can do that.'

'You'll need to do it fast, so that I can follow them. I'm not sure how I'm going to do that yet, but I'll think of something.'

'Okay, but you're right, it'll be tricky. I have no idea where they take the patients, but to follow, well; I would have thought it impossible to do it without being seen.'

'Well, as I said, don't you worry about that, I'll find a way.'

Twelve

The hospital loomed ominously in the beam of her headlights as Helen drove up the driveway and proceeded to park her car at the rear of the building, just outside her living accommodation. A security light flicked on as she pulled up, got out of her car and ran to escape the still heavy downpour.

As she opened the security door she noticed, through the window, the light that had been on in Kate's room suddenly went out. She felt as if her movements were being monitored and it was strange that Kate had been so distant with her that day. She was indeed an odd character and Helen was positive that, however much she wanted to, she was correct in not entirely trusting her yet.

Although she had at first shown some glee, perhaps even excitement, at Helen's contempt for Professor Kirkby's self-proclaimed rules, at the same time, Kate also displayed a degree of loyalty towards him. Helen wondered how far that loyalty went and how it would manifest itself should Kate learn of her suspicions of wrong doing at the hospital. No! She couldn't risk allowing her to discover her and Jenny's plan – not yet, and maybe never.

The feeling of elation at having someone on her side dissipated a little as she unlocked her door and entered the solitary confines of her room. She felt alone again, and despite the promise of help from Jenny, a sudden reality dawned on her that it would be her and no one else who would be taking all the risks. She also wondered if all of her doubts and suspicions were in any way well-founded. She had no real evidence.

It was possible, she thought, that nothing untoward was going on at all and she may end up simply making herself look foolish and paranoid. It might even affect her long-term career prospects. Should that turn out to be the case and she was found snooping and making unwarranted accusations, she would be fortunate ever to find employment in her field of work ever again. Certainly, if all of this happened, there wasn't a hospital in the country that would touch her.

Jenny Cooper, although having witnessed the late night removal of patients from the ward first-hand and with little doubt that something strange was indeed occurring at the hospital, was having much the same thoughts as she arrived home. As she had indicated to Helen, she could not afford to lose her job. She was also scared of the Professor and Sister Thornton. Nevertheless, if there was even the smallest chance that patients were in some way being mistreated, she was unwavering in her promise of help to expose it.

She was also fearful for Helen. Yes, she could do her part in immediately informing her when a patient was removed from the ward, but how on earth would Helen possibly be able to follow undetected? For one thing, she would have to get through the reception without being seen by the prying eyes of Mary, or whoever happened to be on duty at the time. Jenny wasn't sure any of the night-time reception staff were trustworthy, but surely the worst of them, should she be on duty, was Mary.

Helen dried herself off and decided she had to come up with a plan of action to ensure she could, when the time came, successfully follow wherever the next patient was taken. There was no telling when that might be. It might be tomorrow night or a week later, there was no way of knowing as, according to Jenny, there was no fixed pattern. Whenever it happened though, she needed to be prepared rather than simply play it by ear, which could prove to be disastrous.

She was vaguely aware, as she prepared to leave her room once again, of something lingering in the air, a smell she was certain she had smelt before, yet could not place where. An indefinite odour of perfume which she knew was not hers. Had someone been in her room while she was out? She scanned the room for evidence of anything being disturbed, even the bedside drawer where she now kept the diary of Elise Munroe. All seemed exactly as she had left it and she began to relax, the muscles in her neck which had tightened were now looser and at ease once again.

When she arrived at the reception area, all was quiet, as it always seemed to be. She noticed that Mary was not on duty, it was Kathleen this evening, whom when they'd first met, seemed pleasant enough. She took in the layout of the reception hall, the corridors leading off to wards and the doctors' and Professor Kirkby's offices. Her best guess was that the patients, when taken away from the wards in the middle of the night, were taken to Kirkby's office.

It would prove difficult to follow anyone undetected as everywhere was so exposed. It all seemed impossible, yet there had to be a way, and no matter how difficult, she had to find it.

'Good evening, Doctor.' The voice of Kathleen came from the reception hatch. Helen saw the woman leaning towards the glass and peering round at her. Helen walked over to her.

'Good evening,' she said calmly.

'Having a little walkabout?' enquired the woman.

'Yes, just thought I'd look in on my patients.'

'Oh, I see,' she said casually.

'Do you get many disturbances at night? It must be pretty quiet, I imagine.'

'Uh, well yes, it's usually very quiet, yes.'

'Hmm. Anyway, I'd better leave you to your work. Goodnight.'

'Goodnight, Doctor.'

Helen took another glance around the hall, but a solid plan still eluded her. She then went through the door that led to her ward. As she strode confidently down the corridor, she wondered if the nurse on duty tonight would be as friendly, helpful and trustworthy as Jenny had turned out to be. It was then she heard the door she had just come through buzzing loudly behind her. She turned and a silhouetted figure stood perfectly still in the doorway.

'Doctor Ross.'

Helen stood transfixed for a moment before responding.

'Professor Kirkby.'

'Do you mind me asking what are you doing, Helen?'

'I'm carrying out a round of my ward, Professor. Is that okay?'

'A little unusual at this late hour, isn't it?'

'Well, no, at least not where I come from, Professor. It's quite normal.'

'Be that as it may, we don't do things quite the same here as you may have done in London.'

'Well, I don't see…'

'Continue with your round, Helen,' he interjected. 'And I think I'd like to see you in my office first thing tomorrow morning. There are things we need to talk about.'

'As you wish, Professor.'

'Very well, I'll see you at 9 o'clock then. Goodnight Doctor Ross.'

'Goodnight.' She paused for a moment. 'Oh, Professor?'

He turned back to face her. 'Yes?'

'What brings *you* out at this time of night, if you don't mind me asking?'

'This is *my* hospital, Doctor Ross. Night or day, it makes no difference, I like to know what is happening at *all* times. I hope that's clear.'

She nodded. 'Yes, very.'

'Oh, by the way, I hope you enjoyed your meal this evening, Helen.'

'Just a few sandwiches, but yes, thank you, I did. Goodnight Professor.' Having had the last word, she turned swiftly and continued to her ward, yet all the time feeling Kirkby's eyes burning into her back as he continued to stand motionless in the doorway, watching her.

What was he doing there anyway? Helen thought. Had he been tipped off by the receptionist that she was planning on carrying out a round of her ward? Maybe he had a sixth sense.

Either way, it was unnerving and made her realise even more how challenging it would be to unravel the secrets of The Manor.

Helen went through the next door and into her ward. She was still casually dressed from her evening with Jenny, wearing jeans, a sweater and trainers.

'You're early tonight, Professor,' said the nurse in the dimly lit office. Her back was to Helen as she wrote notes at her desk, just as Jenny had been the previous night. When there was no reply, she swivelled round in the chair.

'Early for what?' Helen said.

'I'm sorry, I thought you were…'

'The Professor, I know.'

'Sorry, who are you exactly and what are you doing here? Oh, I'm guessing you must be Doctor Ross.'

'You guessed correctly. And you are?'

'Staff Nurse Jameson.'

'So, you were expecting Professor Kirkby. Any particular reason for that?'

'Uh, well he sometimes pops in at night to check everything is okay, that's all.'

Helen checked her watch. It was 11.30pm. Perhaps Kirkby's appearance was nothing to do with him spying on her. Perhaps she had interrupted one of his scheduled visits to remove one of her patients.

'Really? Well that's exactly what I'm doing. So, *is* everything okay?'

'Yes, everything is quiet and normal. The patients are all sleeping peacefully. No, nothing to report at all really. Sorry about the misunderstanding, you just took me by surprise, that's all.'

Helen offered her a weak smile. 'It's alright, don't worry about it. Now, I'll just take a quiet stroll round the patients if you don't mind.'

'No, of course not. Do you want me to…?'

'No, I'll be fine, thanks. I won't be long.'

Helen ambled past the patients, occasionally taking a look at the charts that hung at the end of each bed. When she came to Maria's bed, she could hear a muffled whimpering. The whimpering became more pronounced as she went closer; Helen clearly saw the bed cover being pulled up around Maria's head, as if she were hiding in real fear.

'There there, shh, it's alright, Maria, it's me, Doctor Ross,' she said, patting her gently on the shoulder. 'What's wrong, what are you afraid of?'

'I thought you were that man – the professor, or that horrible woman,' she said, sniffing, her whole body shaking.

'It's alright, Maria, I'm not going to let anything bad happen to you. I'm your friend; I'm going to help you as I promised. What has the professor been doing to you?'

'He…'

'Is everything alright?' the nurse asked, appearing from nowhere.

Helen spun round to face her. 'Yes, everything's fine,' she said. 'I'm afraid I must have woken her, but she's okay now.'

The nurse came and stood over them suspiciously. Helen leaned close to Maria and whispered. 'Don't worry, I'll see you tomorrow, I promise.' She stood up. 'Right nurse, I'll leave you to it.'

'Thank you,' the nurse said cynically, followed by a curt, almost dismissive, 'goodnight Doctor.'

As Helen arrived back in the reception hall, she took one last glance around her. The task she had set herself still seemed near impossible to achieve. She decided to sleep on it. She had no idea on which night the call would come from Jenny, but she had to be prepared. For all she knew, that call could come as soon as tomorrow night, when Jenny was next on duty.

She walked back to her room and thought about Maria's words. In her mind, there was now little doubt that something sinister was taking place at the hospital. It also seemed likely that at least some of the staff were in collusion with the professor and his night-time visits – she was sure that Nurse Jameson was, and almost certainly some of the reception staff. Jenny seemed to be the only person she felt she could fully trust, and though she hoped she was wrong, she was now even beginning to have serious doubts about Kate.

By the time she got herself into bed, it was around midnight. She felt exhausted, both physically and mentally, yet she could not find sleep. The fear in Maria's eyes and the sound of her voice haunted her. She felt powerless. Had she got in the way tonight? Was the professor's appearance more than a coincidence? She strongly suspected that had she not been there, Maria or one of the other patients would have been dragged from their beds and taken somewhere. If that were the case, then by being there, she may have done some good, perhaps.

She knew though, that it was only delaying the inevitable; it was only a matter of time before the professor tried again. For all she knew, he may be at this very moment, knowing that the coast was clear, removing a patient. These thoughts and more kept her awake all night and the heavy rain that spattered loudly against her window only made matters worse, so that come the morning she was exhausted and had a full-blown headache. The thought of her meeting with Kirkby only served to increase the tension in her head and neck. Normally she would relish such a meeting, but at this moment she dreaded it.

Thirteen

Helen had given up trying to sleep; it was proving impossible. She glanced at her bedside clock, it was only 6am but there was little point in staying in bed. She sat on the bed and massaged her temples for a moment before switching on the coffee machine.

Breakfast was served in the dining room anywhere between seven and eight and, on this morning, considering she'd only had a few sandwiches at the pub the night before, she thought it wise to partake. It might even make her feel better; help her to keep body and soul together during her meeting with Kirkby, she thought.

Two cups of coffee, some painkillers and a long, hot shower later, she began to feel a little more ready for the day ahead, whatever it might bring. She no longer had the dread she'd felt about seeing Professor Kirkby and positively relished the coming night, when she hoped that something would happen and Jenny would call her. It could end up being another long night, but this time, she thought, it might just be worthwhile.

There were only a couple of doctors having breakfast when Helen arrived at the dining hall. Doctors Brownlow and Schmitt were both devouring eggs and bacon. Helen sat opposite them in the seat that Kirkby had allocated for her on the day of her arrival. It seemed so long ago now. David Brownlow smiled and greeted her as she sat down.

'Good morning, Helen, did you sleep well?'

'Good morning. No, not terribly well as a matter of fact.'

'Oh dear, sorry to hear that. Well, it's nice to see you at breakfast. I'm sure a hearty full English will set you up for the day.'

'Yes, I'm sure it will.'

At that point a member of the kitchen staff appeared, carrying a tray with a pre-prepared cooked breakfast; pots of coffee and tea were already on the table. The woman set the hot plate down and left.

'So, Helen, is the invitation to dinner at the local hostelry still open?' asked David Brownlow with a smile.

'Yes, of course.'

'Wonderful, I'll…'

'But not tonight I'm afraid, she interrupted. 'I plan to catch up on my sleep. Maybe another night?'

'Oh, yes, of course, I understand.'

'So, Doctor Schmitt, how long have you been at the hospital?' Helen asked, changing the subject.

The woman spoke timidly and with a hint of a German accent. 'Not very long, about six months, I suppose.'

'Do you like it here?'

She hesitated for a moment. 'Yes, it is good.' She took a last sip of coffee then raised herself from the chair. 'Please excuse me, I have to go now.' And with that she left the dining room. She seemed uncomfortable and awkward and almost bumped into Kate as she entered the room.

'Morning, Kate,' Helen said.

'Morning, how are you?'

'I'm okay, thanks. How are you? Feeling better today?'

'Better?'

'You were suffering a little yesterday – a headache?'

'Oh yes. Yes I'm fine,' she said, taking a seat next to Helen. 'I'm sorry if I seemed off with you. You know how it is when you have a thumping headache, I was pretty tense.'

'Don't be silly, I understand. Where's the professor anyway? Doesn't he have breakfast?'

'Not always, no, sometimes he takes it in his room. You went out again yesterday evening then?'

'Yes, that's right,' Helen said cagily.

'The Drunken Duck again?'

'Yes.' Helen leaned towards Kate. 'Was anything said by Kirkby?' she asked in a hushed voice.

'No, not really. He did seem in a foul mood though. Look, Helen, it's none of my business, but maybe you should humour him a little – at least until you've been here a while longer.'

'Yes, maybe you're right, Kate. Maybe I should.'

Doctor Brownlow, at the opposite side of the table, wiped his mouth with his napkin, took a last sip of tea and got up, seemingly annoyed at their private conversation. 'Good morning ladies,' he said, and then left.

'Oh dear, what's wrong with him?' Helen asked.

Kate shrugged her shoulders. 'Fuck knows – I wouldn't worry about it.'

'I won't, Doctor Brownlow's the least of my worries.'

Kate turned to look at her. 'What do you mean?'

'Oh nothing, just a figure of speech,' she said, finishing her meal. 'Well, I'll leave you to have your breakfast in peace. I have an appointment with Kirkby.'

'Oh, what about? What have you done now?'

'Nothing that I know about. That is, apart from missing out on a couple of dinners and carrying out a round of my ward last night. If either of those are a crime, then I'm guilty.'

'Look, Helen…' She paused for a moment. 'Just tread carefully. Don't upset him.'

'That sounds like a warning of sorts to me.'

'Just friendly advice.'

Helen smiled. 'Thanks, I'll bear it in mind.'

'Yes, do.'

She wished Kate would open up to her. It seemed that on a couple of occasions she had wanted to tell Helen something, but then at the last moment held back.

It was almost nine when she arrived at Professor Kirkby's office. She took a deep breath and knocked on the door.

'Come!' came a muffled voice through the heavy oak door.

Helen entered his office.

'Doctor Ross, good morning. Please, take a seat,' he said calmly from behind his desk. He looked up from his work, a feigned smile on his face. 'How did the round of your ward go last night? No problems I hope?'

'No, no problems. I'm quite concerned about one patient in particular though.'

'Don't tell me – Maria. Am I correct?'

'Yes, you are, Professor.'

'I thought so.' He got up from his chair, moved closer to Helen and sat on the corner of his desk, looking down at her. He sighed. 'Helen, Helen, Helen, *what* – am I going to do with you?'

'I'm sorry, I don't follow.'

'Don't you?'

'No, I'm afraid not.'

'You came here from a fancy London hospital. I fully understand it may have been different to our humble establishment, but the fact is, we're doing good work here. You'll see that in time. Maria is a difficult case, I grant you, but she's responding well to the treatment given before your arrival. All I'm saying is, why not see how it goes? After all, you've only been here a few days, and... Well, maybe you should give yourself a little more time to settle in before...'

'With all due respect, Professor, she's my patient and I'd like to deal with her in my own way. I'd also like to speak to my predecessor, Doctor Munroe, about her if possible. Would you happen to know where she is now?'

'No,' he said, standing up, his irritation with Helen now very much to the fore once again.

'Do you mean, no, you don't know where she is?'

'That's correct. Now, I won't keep you any longer,' he said, returning to his seat. 'Good morning to you, Doctor.'

Considering herself dismissed, almost admonished, she stood up to leave the office. But before she did, she turned back to face him.

'Do you still require me to attend the 10 o'clock meeting?'

'That won't be necessary,' he replied dispassionately, as he flicked through some papers.

She couldn't help feeling he was hiding something. In fact, it seemed to her that almost everyone at the hospital was hiding something. He was particularly evasive, she thought, regarding Elise Munroe and her whereabouts. Where was she? What had become of her? Had she retired and slipped into obscurity? Helen had to find out.

∞∞∞∞

The day passed with Helen seeing more of her patients on a one to one basis in her office. Without exception, all were suffering from paranoid delusions, as apparently was Maria Dobson. The interesting thing was, with all of them, they had been at the hospital for some months and had shown no signs of improvement whatsoever. This, she thought, was unusual.

There was, however, a vast difference between them and Maria, they all appeared completely out of touch with reality whereas Maria definitely seemed very much in touch and aware of her predicament.

Helen took lunch and dinner with the other staff members; she was amiable towards the professor and engaged in polite, non-work orientated conversation, yet there wasn't a moment when she didn't feel a loathing behind his eyes. After dinner she retired to her room for an hour or so of sleep. It could be a long night again, should she receive the call from Jenny. There was, of course, the possibility that nothing would happen, yet in a perverse kind of way she hoped something would.

It was around 11pm when she woke.

She'd had no contact with Jenny since their meeting the previous evening and though she sympathised, she hoped her friend would not become so afraid that she wouldn't go through with their plan. Helen had thought about the problem of following the professor, Sister Thornton, or both, through the corridors in the middle of the night, and was now as prepared as she could ever hope to be.

She threw on a comfortable pair of jeans and a dark roll-neck sweater, walked along the corridor, through the reception and down the next corridor to her office. There she would wait, and hope that tonight would be the night. The pre-arranged signal was that Jenny would give two rings on the phone in Helen's room should something occur.

Helen needed to let Jenny know that the arrangement had changed, and that when, or if the time came, she should call her office phone instead. She picked up the phone and dialled the extension for the ward.

A voice answered.

'Jenny?'

'No, this is Nurse Jameson. Is that you, Doctor Ross?'

'Yes. Where's Jenny?'

'She couldn't make it in tonight, I'm afraid. I'm standing in for her. Can I help you with anything?'

'Uh, no, that's okay. Thank you.'

She suddenly had a sick feeling in the pit of her stomach. Was Jenny ill, or had she simply decided not to become involved? Either way, it looked as if she was now on her own. They had exchanged their mobile numbers at the pub; Helen searched her contacts and rang the number. It rang and rang until it went to voicemail. Helen left a brief message, asking if she was alright and for her to call as soon as possible. The nauseous sensation in her stomach only increased. There was something wrong - she could feel it.

Like a fire, a deep sense of anxiety began to spread through her entire body. There was no logic, no foundation for the unease she felt, yet something about the situation troubled her profoundly. Her muscles tensed, her head throbbed, her heart thumped and leapt. What had happened to Jenny? Had she forsaken her? Was Helen's judgement of her wrong? For a moment it seemed she could not trust or rely on anyone but herself. But what if something bad had happened to Jenny?

She sat in complete darkness at her desk and attempted, with a degree of success, to control her breathing. As she began to feel calmer once again, she put her feet up on the desk, closed her eyes and soon dozed off.

∞∞∞∞

Jenny had not seen her attacker. It all happened so fast. She had been preparing a light meal before getting ready for work when it happened. The portable T.V she was watching in the kitchen drowned out any sound of the person who crept up behind her. Before she had a chance to run or defend herself, the assailant's hands grabbed her throat and squeezed until she collapsed onto the floor.

It happened only an hour or so before she was due to be on duty at The Manor. When she came to, she coughed and spluttered, her throat was painful and she couldn't speak. She just lay there for a moment, sprawled face down on the kitchen floor, as her cat brushed past her.

After raising herself up, it took her some time to grasp the reality of what had happened. But why? Why would someone enter her home and attack her like this? For a while she sat and wept. She examined herself in the mirror. Her throat was red and sore, whoever had done this was powerful and strong. She felt herself lucky to be alive.

She could still barely speak when she called the police, but somehow managed to give her name and address. They could tell she was in some distress and attended shortly after, insisting she go to hospital to be checked out, but she would have none of it, insisting that she was perfectly alright.

The police officers checked her cottage from top to bottom, there was nothing missing and no sign of a break-in, which led them to believe it was a purely random attack. There was little or no crime in the area and, at the time of the attack, the back door to her cottage had been unlocked as always.

They stayed with her for an hour and a half, and told her that a statement could wait until the next day when her voice had recovered. In the meantime she should keep all windows and doors securely locked.

It was almost midnight and, with all that had happened, it was only now she thought of work and the commitment she had made to Helen. Feeling a little better now, and also nervous of being alone for the night, she locked up, got in her car and drove to The Manor.

Fourteen

The black thunder clouds rolled over the night sky ominously as Jenny drove the six miles to the hospital. She felt ill at ease and kept imagining someone being in the back seat, ready to attack her again. It was, she knew, quite an illogical fear; nevertheless, she was glad to see the driveway that led up to The Manor come into view.

She went straight to the ward and to the office where Nurse Jameson was sat drinking tea.

'Jenny! What are you doing here?'

'Sorry I'm late,' she said, her voice rasping, 'had a spot of bother, but you can go home now.'

'What's happened? You sound terrible.'

'It's a long story. I'll tell you all about it tomorrow. You go home now – I'm fine. Thanks for standing in for me – I'll make it up to you.'

'Are you sure?'

'Absolutely.'

'Well – alright then, if you insist.' The nurse collected her personal belongings and put her coat on. 'By the way, Doctor Ross was looking for you earlier, I daresay she's asleep now, but when she called, it was from her office extension.'

'Oh, right, thanks; I'm sure it can wait until tomorrow, whatever it was. Goodnight then.'

'Goodnight, Jenny,' she said with a quizzical tone.

As soon as she had gone, Jenny dialled out the extension

number for Helen's living quarters – there was no answer. She hung up and tried her office.

Helen, still in darkness, jumped when her phone rang. She had no idea what the time was or why anyone would be calling her. The anxiety flooded back almost immediately on waking. She fumbled for the desk lamp, switched it on, composed herself and picked up the handset.

'Yes?' she said drowsily.

A still rasping voice answered. 'Helen, its Jenny.'

'Jenny! My God, where have you been? I've been worried about you. What's wrong with your voice?'

'Well, let's just say I'm lucky to be alive. Someone got into my house, sneaked up on me and tried to strangle me.'

Helen sat bolt upright in her chair. 'Oh my God! Are you okay?'

'Yes, I'm fine. My throat hurts a bit still, but apart from that…'

'Do you know who it was? Have they caught the person?'

'No, I didn't see anyone. Whoever it was came up from behind. I'm sure they're long gone now; they haven't a snowball's chance of catching them. The police think it was just a random attack.'

'Random? Was it, I wonder.'

'What do you mean?'

'Jenny, have you told anyone, anyone at all about our plans?'

'No, no one. Oh, come on, surely you don't think...?'

'I don't know what to think,' she said, pacing the office, 'but doesn't it seem awfully coincidental to you?'

'I hadn't thought about it. But as I said, I've told no one.'

She paused momentarily. 'No, I'm sorry, Helen, I can't believe it, it's just too incredible, even if there is something going on here, surely it can't be worth killing someone for?'

Helen sighed. 'Maybe you're right; maybe I'm seeing things that aren't there. I'm just glad you're alright.'

'Do you still want me to call you if something happens?'

'I don't know. I'm not sure I want to involve you anymore. If something happened to you or you lost your job, I'd never forgive myself.'

'Nothing's going to happen to me, Helen. I want to do this.'

'Well, if you're sure, but don't take any unnecessary risks, okay?'

'No, I'll be very careful.'

'I'm going to stay in my office. It seems to me the only way of following without being seen. Call my mobile as soon as you can if anything happens.'

'Right, will do.'

Helen switched off her desk lamp so that no light would show under her office door, sat back in her chair again and waited.

∞∞∞∞

It was almost 1.30am when Sister Thornton arrived at the ward. She was clearly taken aback to see Jenny in charge.

'Nurse Cooper, I was under the impression Nurse Jameson was standing in for you tonight.'

'Yes, I'm sorry for being late, Sister. I was feeling rather ill, but I'm alright now,' she said.

'I see – very commendable I'm sure.'

'Sister,' she said, and then paused, unsure of whether she should continue. 'Do you mind me asking what treatment the patients receive when they are taken from the ward late at night? I mean…'

'It's nothing that concerns you,' Sister Thornton snapped. 'Professor Kirkby knows what he is doing and that's all you need to know. Now, get a wheelchair for me, I'll be taking Maria for treatment tonight.'

'Very good, Sister.'

While Jenny fetched a wheelchair, Sister Thornton approached Maria's bed. She took the syringe from her pocket, slid off the protective cover and injected the serum into Maria's arm. She flinched only briefly as the needle entered, and then, although conscious, she appeared quite calm.

Jenny returned with a wheelchair and assisted Sister Thornton to lift Maria out of bed and into it. The sister then strapped her in and took her away.

Helen woke with a start as her mobile phone vibrated on her desk. She picked it up immediately and answered the call.

'Thornton has just this moment taken Maria Dobson, she's probably heading your way,' Jenny said excitedly.

'Okay, this is it, then.'

'Please be careful, Helen. Call me to let me know you're alright.'

'I will. Better go, I think I can hear her coming along the corridor now.'

'Take care,' Jenny said, but Helen had already hung up and

was poised, listening and waiting. She could hear the faint, eerie squeak of the wheelchair being slowly pushed along the corridor and then passing by her door.

After it had passed, she slowly opened her door and peered along the dimly lit corridor to see Sister Thornton turning left and by-passing the professor's office. It was now or never. She left the safety of her office and made her way quietly along the corridor, following the continuous squeaking of the wheelchair.

She arrived at the point where the woman had turned and peered around the corner. She now observed the sister turning off again, this time to her right. Helen had not been in this part of the hospital before. She followed again until she reached the next junction.

She held her position yet again and watched as Sister Thornton entered an elevator. Once she was inside, Helen moved towards the elevator and saw it was going down. How could she follow now? Certainly not by using the same lift; she could find herself running straight into her.

It could only be leading to a basement, but in such an old building, surely there must also be some stairs, she thought. She moved further along the corridor. This part of the building gave her the creeps even more than the rest of the hospital, but she had no intention of giving up now, not when she was so close to getting some answers.

She found a solid, but dusty old door at the very end of the corridor. It had to be the way down to the basement. She carefully tried the rusty handle. The door creaked open and through the murk she could just make out a narrow stone staircase. But where and what would it ultimately lead her to?

Helen took a deep breath and stepped inside. She fumbled around for a light switch but couldn't find one; the staircase was in complete and utter darkness. The bare brick walls were cold and damp as, with both hands, she felt her way down the steep and narrow passage. She stopped for a moment; there it was again, that sick feeling in the pit of her stomach, a feeling of deep anxiety that wanted to control her mind and body.

She breathed deeply again, this time holding it before slowly breathing out, this she repeated a couple of times before continuing her descent. Her progress was slow; the steps were narrow and slippery and made all the worse by being in complete darkness. After what seemed a long time, however, the steps ended and she found herself on level ground.

Pausing for a moment, she listened carefully. There was uncertainty in her mind as to whether or not she was imagining it, but she could have sworn that for a moment she could hear the faint sound of music playing. She shuffled, feeling her way closer to where she thought the sound was coming from.

A few steps later she reached the end of the passage and, losing her footing, almost stumbled against what was clearly a door. She froze for a moment. Could someone have heard her? As the moments passed, it seemed she was safe. And now she could hear the music clearly. She had not imagined it, it was real, a classical harpsichord piece by whom she thought she recognised as Bach.

Then, above the sound of the music, she heard it, the unnervingly calm voice of Professor Kirkby, and although she could not make out the words, it was apparent he was talking to someone – perhaps Maria, or Sister Thornton.

Helen fumbled around for a door handle and found one. But what to do next? She hadn't thought this far ahead and now she was faced with a decision to either retreat the way she had come, or to enter the room and find out exactly what was going on. After a moment of deliberation and another deep breath, she chose the latter.

She twisted the old-fashioned latch and carefully pushed the door so there was a small gap. It wasn't enough to see anything, so she pushed a little more. This time though, the door groaned on its rusty hinges.

'Come in, Helen, I've been expecting you,' came the voice of the Professor.

Small droplets of perspiration formed on her forehead, her heartrate increased, she could feel it thumping in her chest rapidly. She felt like running back up the dark stairwell, getting in her car and getting as far away as possible. But something stopped her – the promise of help she had made to Maria.

She pushed the door open wider and stepped into the cavernous basement. Apart from a light that was concentrated on Maria, still strapped into her wheelchair, the room was in darkness and Helen could not see the professor or Sister Thornton. But then he stepped out of the shadowy recesses and into the light.

'How nice of you to join us, my dear. As I said, I've been expecting you. It has become very clear to me over the past few days that you are indeed a most tenacious young lady.

And now I suppose you would like to know what I'm doing down here with your patient – correct?'

As always, his manner was intimidating, but although her mouth was dry, she found the courage to speak. 'The thought had crossed my mind, yes.'

'Well then, please allow me to enlighten you. Don't be afraid, come in my dear.'

Helen ventured further into the room. She approached Maria. Her head was slumped.

'Don't worry, she's perfectly alright. The drug will soon wear off and she'll be fully awake again,' the professor said, walking slowly over to Helen.

'So Professor, enlighten me,' she said confidently, 'what exactly is going on here?'

'Helen, my work here is, how shall I put it – unconventional, I know, but generally for the greater good. You see, for many years I worked in a secret government establishment…'

'Porton Down,' Helen interjected.

He looked surprised. 'That's quite correct.' He paused before continuing. 'I was involved in certain investigations concerning the human mind and its weaknesses. It was my job to exploit those weaknesses for reasons of…'

'Yes?'

'National security, of course. We were working on ways to manipulate the minds of enemies of the state and make them work willingly for us instead. Unfortunately, my department was closed down – it was deemed by some as being unethical.'

'What kind of investigations exactly?' Helen noticed the

shadowy figure of Sister Thornton appearing from the darkness.

'Don't say any more, Professor,' said the woman, sharply, 'she won't listen, she certainly won't understand. She's been nothing but trouble since she arrived here.'

'Now now, Sister, I think we at least owe Doctor Ross an explanation. Besides, once she realises the good work we're doing here, she may even wish to join us. Isn't that right, Helen?'

'Who knows? Maybe,' she lied. 'So, you were saying, Professor?'

'Yes, of course. Well, I don't have to remind you that since 9/11, we have been in what is a state of war against terrorism. There are other threats as well, of course, threats that are every bit as terrifying: Russia, China, even crime. Don't believe everything you read in the newspapers or see on the television about crime rates dropping. It's much worse than ever, believe me.'

'So what's your point, Professor?'

'We were working on mind altering drugs, along with therapy, to get to grips with all of these threats. We were making headway too, until a few do-gooders marched in and stopped our funding. Then I found myself out of a job, until the post of Residential Professor arose here.'

Helen glared at him. 'That still doesn't explain what you're doing here.'

'Continuing the work. Someone has to.'

'You're using patients as guinea-pigs? Brainwashing them?'

'For the greater good, my dear. For the greater good.'

Helen shook her head, unable to believe what she was hearing. 'You're quite mad,' she finally said, glancing at Maria, sedated in the wheelchair, her head flopping on her shoulder.

'No Helen, don't you understand? This work has to continue, no matter what.'

'And what happens to the patients once you have done with them and completed your sordid experiments?'

Sister Thornton moved towards Helen and grabbed her arm. She was much bigger and stronger and Helen could not release herself from the grip. 'Enough of this, Professor. I told you she wouldn't co-operate,' she said firmly.

Helen, struggling to free herself, shouted at the professor. 'Who's in charge here? You or her?'

Kirkby looked at Helen thoughtfully for a moment. 'I'm afraid Sister Thornton is quite right, you won't join us, will you? Certainly not without a great deal more…' he chuckled to himself, 'a great deal more persuasion.'

Helen, pinned to the wall by the sister, stopped struggling. 'Are all of the doctors in on this?'

'Most of them, yes. They can see what I'm trying to achieve, you see.'

'Kate?'

'Enough questions, Helen.'

'And what about Nurse Cooper? Did you have something to do with her attempted murder?'

The professor chuckled again. 'Ah, Nurse Cooper. Yes, our spy in the village told me of your little meeting in the pub. We can't have loose ends, Helen, speaking of which…'

'I suppose Elise Munroe was a loose end as well.'

'Yes, she was, just like you. However, despite our shaky start, I had high hopes for you, Helen – I still do. Oh well, it can't be helped, I suppose. If you're not going to join us of your own free will, there seems little choice.' He turned to the sister. 'Perhaps you would like to assist Doctor Ross and make her comfortable.'

Fifteen

Helen turned her head away from the bright glare of the lamp. She struggled to move her arms but they were clamped at the wrists to the chair Sister Thornton had strapped her to. Her legs, too, were bound at the ankles, and a thick strap around her chest made it difficult to breathe. She flicked her eyes up at the professor, desperate for him to look at her so she could plead with him to let her go. How she was going to do that, she wasn't quite sure, as the tape across her mouth was fixed tight. She watched as he pulled back slowly on the syringe then tapped it against his palm before lifting it to his eyes to study it.

'All ready,' he said, turning to Sister Thornton. 'Would you like to do the honours, or shall I?'

Helen cried out, but her throaty scream dissolved against the tape. She thrashed about in the chair, her restraints preventing her from moving more than a few inches. Sister Thornton laughed and Helen glared at her, willing her to look into her eyes.

'She's all yours,' the sister said, urging the professor to continue.

Helen felt a firm grip on her forearm and then the sharp prick of a needle in her wrist. She clenched her fist, feeling the icy serum seeping up through her arm and into her shoulder. Within moments, a thick, syrupy feeling washed over her and her mind fogged. The last thing she remembered was the shadowy forms of both the professor and the sister standing over her, smiles dancing on their faces.

When she came to, she was instantly aware of a slow, rhythmic pounding in her head; the blood pulsating against her skull. It took her a few moments to realise she was no longer restrained, but laying on a mattress in the corner of the same, dank room she had been in previously. She had no idea how much time had passed and she flicked her eyes around for clues, but the same lamp emitted its harsh glow in the centre of the room, and there was no sign of a window, or daylight. She could have been out for minutes or hours, and not knowing terrified her. But what terrified her even more was not knowing what she had been injected with. Mind-altering drugs, the professor had spoken about. She closed her eyes and took a deep breath, trying to establish if she felt any different. She felt weak and ill, yes. And she ached, her head especially. But other than that...

'Helen! You're awake. I trust you had a good sleep?' Turning her head, she saw Professor Kirkby standing in the doorway, a white, metal case in his hands. She watched as he closed and locked the door, then strode towards her, his face expressionless. 'So, how are you feeling?'

'What have you done to me?' she hissed, ignoring his question. 'Let me out of here!'

'I'm afraid I can't allow that. We have more work to do. You will join us, Helen. Soon you won't want to leave.'

'When you've destroyed my brain, you mean.'

The professor chuckled. 'My dear Helen, I have no intention

of destroying your brain. What possible use would you be to me then, hmm? Besides, the last injection was nothing more than a sedative and muscle relaxant – quite harmless.'

She didn't know if she believed him or not, but it was true, her mind felt normal enough. For some reason, though, Helen could not move. She felt powerless and terrified. 'What about the patients? You're giving them far more than sedatives. Without their consent you're experimenting on them, you're...'

'Not experimenting, Helen. Merely investigating. And observing. There's a difference. I told you yesterday...'

'Yesterday?' Helen glared at him. 'How long have I been out?'

The professor glanced at his watch. 'About eleven hours,' he said, flicking open the catch on his case. 'Anyway, as I was saying, you have to understand that this work is vital, Helen. Do you not care about the security of your country?'

'Of course I do!' she said, 'but you can't just conduct your...your *experiments* on unwitting people, people who are unable to voice their consent. It's wrong! It's unethical! It's monstrous!'

The professor shook his head and perched on the edge of the bed. 'Helen, please.' He turned his head to look at her. 'The patients at this hospital have severe mental disorders, and as you are more than aware, there are inadequate provisions for them in mainstream society. They are far safer here than they are trying to carve some sort of life in a community that has no place for them. Do you not agree?'

Helen shifted on the bed in an attempt to sit up, but fell back against the pillows. 'You're twisting everything,' she snapped. 'I'm not suggesting they should be walking the streets, I'm suggesting...no, *telling* you, that what you are doing is a disgusting and sickening abuse of their human rights!'

Helen saw the professor's eyes move towards the far corner of the room. He nodded his head and Sister Thornton arrived at his side. She held Helen's shoulders as the professor removed a syringe from his case.

'Answer me!' she yelled, writhing under the firm grip of the sister. 'How can you even justify this? You're sick! Both of you!'

She felt the needle enter her arm, but in moments the deep feeling of anger and fear was replaced by a calmness, the like of which she had never experienced before.

Sixteen

'You need to eat, Helen.' The professor nudged the plate of toast towards her and smiled. 'Just a bite or two, it'll make you feel so much better.'

'I'm really not hungry, Professor,' she said, pushing it away.

He flattened the sheets and sat down on the bed. 'Helen,' he said, removing the plate and placing it on the bedside table, 'when you're ready - and only when you're ready - we need to talk.'

She propped herself up on the pillows. 'What day is it?'

'It's Thursday,' he said, holding out a glass of water. Helen took it, raised it to her lips and gulped half of it down before passing it back to him. Was it Monday or Tuesday when she'd first discovered them in the basement? The fog in her head rolled and shifted.

'I'll leave you to rest,' he said, 'you've had a long morning. But I'll be back later.' He took the plate of uneaten toast, stood up, and strolled to the door, turning back briefly to look at her. 'You're doing well, Helen; very well. Keep it up.'

Helen dozed and was only disturbed once when Sister Thornton delivered her a fresh jug of water. She said nothing, just watched as the sister placed it on the bedside table and left. Now, though, with her head clearer, she was sat upright, the jug of water empty, and waiting impatiently for the professor's return. She wasn't sure how much time had passed – it was difficult to tell – but when he arrived some time later, she was glad of the disruption from the monotony of it all.

'You're looking well, dear,' he said. 'It's good to see you so...' he paused for a moment, looking at her, '...so refreshed.' Helen nodded, motioning for him to sit down, and he obliged, taking a seat on the edge of her bed.

'Yes, I do feel better', she said. 'Much better.'

'Good, good.' The professor studied her for a moment, his face impassive, as it always was. 'I'd like to talk about *you*, Helen, about your professionalism and the good work - I believe – that you can bring to our research here.' Helen nodded, urging him to continue. 'You came highly recommended, you know.'

'As a psychiatrist, perhaps,' she said. 'But I have no experience with...' she paused, and looked at him. 'What, exactly is it I'll be doing?'

'There's no need to worry about that for the moment. What's important right now is for me to ensure you appreciate the importance of my...investigations.'

'Oh, I do,' Helen said. 'I didn't at first, but now you've taken the time to explain it to me fully, well, I think what you're doing is remarkable.'

'Good,' he said, not taking his eyes off her. 'I'm still slightly concerned about your earlier outburst regarding the welfare of the patients. Would you care to talk about that?'

'I was wrong, and I apologise. I can see now that making the patients compliant for your own research has its added benefits.'

'And they are?'

'A working environment that isn't disruptive,' she said,

meeting his gaze. 'And an added sense of security for the staff.'

'And for the patients themselves?'

She thought for a moment. 'They're at peace, Professor. Finally. And they've been given a purpose. A sense of usefulness, of belonging. Of being a part of something that one day will be recognised as...' She paused. 'It will be recognised one day, won't it, Professor?'

He laughed. 'Of course it will!' He stood up, strode to the end of the bed, and placed both his hands on the footboard, leaning forward. 'One day, Helen, you are going to be so glad you met me.'

Helen swung her legs off the side of the bed. She was stiff and achy from having spent so much time immobile, but her mind was clear. Just as the professor had claimed, the after-effects of the drugs seemed to be minimal. The patients, he'd said, experienced nothing more than weariness that lasted just a few days. And with each new study, their anxiety and reluctance to participate lessoned to such a degree that they became visibly content with the proceedings.

'About Maria,' the professor said, as Helen got to her feet. 'She's still in the early stages of treatment. You'll continue to see an improvement in her behaviour over the next few weeks.'

Helen nodded.

'Well, I can see you're keen to get started. I'll have Sister Thornton escort you to your room.'

A Few Weeks Later

'Good evening, Professor, it's a lovely night.'

'Yes, isn't it,' he said, gesturing for Helen to take a seat alongside him at the dining table. She nodded her greeting at the other doctors before pulling out her chair and sitting down. 'Now,' he said, ensuring she was comfortable, 'before we begin, I'd just like to say, and I'm sure we're all agreed, how sorry I am that Doctor Schmitt has left us. I'm sure we all wish her the best in her future endeavours...whatever they may be.' There was a slight chuckle from the far end of the table and the corners of the professor's lips rose in a half smile.

'Yes, indeed, here-here!' Doctor Brownlow added cheerfully.

'And on a lighter note, I was wondering if anyone would like to have a few rounds of bridge with me after dinner.'

'I'd love to,' Helen said. Doctor Wright and David Brownlow promptly followed in making up the numbers.

'Wonderful! I'll look forward to that immensely. Right,' he said, picking up his spoon and sliding his soup bowl towards him. 'Let's eat, shall we?'

Helen ate in silence, her thoughts very much on how her colleagues' behaviour towards her had changed over the past two weeks. There hadn't been any real animosity before, but simple gestures – the offering of a bread roll or a drink, the holding open of a door, the courteous greetings as they passed each other in the hospital corridors – had made her feel less alien, somehow. The people around the table had no family; no place to go; nothing to distract them from their work at the hospital. She wondered if that was why the professor had employed her – that it was the ticking of the "single" and "no dependents" boxes on her application form, rather than her experience, that had landed her the job. Yes, she thought; that made perfect sense.

'Helen, cold soup isn't the most pleasant thing to eat.'

She looked up at the professor and then down into her bowl where a thin skin was settling on its surface.

'Sorry, I was miles away,' she said, dunking in her spoon and giving it a stir. 'Tell me, what happens here at Christmas? Can I help decorate?'

After dinner, Professor Kirkby took Helen by the arm as she stood to leave the table.

'Could you hang on one moment?' he said, 'I'd like to have a quiet word.'

'Of course.' Helen took her seat again, slightly worried that something was amiss. The professor had been fine during breakfast and lunch and she hadn't, to her knowledge, done anything wrong. Still, she had an uneasy feeling in her stomach as they waited for the other doctors to leave the dining hall.

'I'm so glad you're settling in at last, my dear. I can't tell you how pleased I am with you. Later tonight, I would like to continue working on Maria. I was wondering if you'd care to assist me.'

Helen looked at him expectantly. 'Yes, Professor, I'd like that. If you think I'm ready, of course.'

'More than ready. I've been looking forward to this moment; to get you on board properly. We'll discuss the details over bridge, if that's okay.'

Helen smiled. 'I hope I don't embarrass myself like I did last time,' she said. 'I'm afraid I'm a bit of a slow learner.'

'Nonsense!' He got to his feet. 'If the mind is empty, it is ready for anything.' He placed an arm on her shoulder. 'It's so good to have you with us, Helen. So good. Now, if you'll excuse me...'

A few hours later, having lost at bridge and with the professor's instructions clear in her mind, Helen made her way to Ward Ten. She hadn't walked this particular corridor, nor visited her ward, since the time she'd spent with the professor in his investigating suite, as he liked to call it. She had no idea who would be on duty – the nurses never dined with them – but she suspected that as it was a weekday, Jenny would be there. As she turned the corner and glanced at the reception desk, she realised her thoughts had been correct; there was no mistaking her. They hadn't seen one another in two weeks and, as Helen approached, the fluttering in her stomach increased.

'Jenny, she said. Anything to report?'

Jenny spun around in her chair. 'Helen!' She sprang to her feet and practically danced around the edge of her desk to join her. 'Where the hell have you been? I was so worried about you!' She flung her arms around Helen's neck and gripped her in a tight hug. 'My God, what happened? I thought I'd never see you again. I thought...'

'I'm perfectly fine,' Helen said firmly, easing herself backwards and away from her. 'There's absolutely nothing to worry about. I'm a bit rushed, to be honest, so could you just get me a wheelchair for...'

'Hang on!' Jenny said. 'You can't just stroll in here as if nothing's happened, as if we...'

'Nurse!' Helen snapped. 'A wheelchair, please.'

Jenny glared at her and then, when Helen's expression remained hostile, she backed away and strode to the other end of the ward. She returned moments later, her face sombre. 'What's going on, Helen?' she whispered, manoeuvring the chair in front of her. 'You can talk to me, you know you can.'

'There's nothing to talk about,' Helen said. 'Nothing at all.'

'But what about Kirkby? About everything that's going on?' She side-stepped so she was facing Helen directly, and gripped her arm. 'What about everything we talked about?'

Helen shook her off, released the brake on the chair, and moved forwards, heading for the double doors, which would lead her to her patients.

'Wait!' Jenny said, her voice almost a shriek as she raced up beside her. 'I deserve some sort of explanation, surely? You can't just...'

Helen stopped in her tracks. 'Jenny, in case you've forgotten, I'm your superior. I can do anything I want. But, to answer your question, I got it wrong, okay? The work Professor Kirkby is doing is incredible. I didn't understand it then, but I do now. So please...' she turned the chair '...just do as I ask and we'll say no more about it.'

Maria's bed was at the far end of the ward, directly beneath the window that overlooked the vast expanse of the hospital grounds. They approached her quietly, passing five other patients whose motionless bodies were slumped heavily in their beds. The intermittent squeak of the wheelchair was the only noise interrupting the silence.

'Roll up her sleeve, please,' Helen said quietly, wheeling the chair to a standstill.

Jenny hesitated, glared at Helen and, faced with nothing but a frosty stare, fumbled with Maria's nightclothes. Once her arm was free, she took the syringe from Helen and, as ordered, injected her.

Helen left with Maria Dobson strapped into the wheelchair, her head flopping down to one side, her body limp. She entered the lift that took them down to the basement, to where the professor and Sister Thornton eagerly awaited their arrival.

Seventeen

'It's just not good enough! We can't have patients just laying around in soiled sheets!' Helen yanked at Jenny's arm, pushing her out of the corridor. 'I suggest you get this sorted out right now!'

'It was just a splash of water,' Jenny protested, as she found herself hurtling through the door of the laundry room. 'It was right at the corner of his bed. I didn't mean to...'

'Jenny!' Helen whispered, shoving her up against the towel bales. 'I've got it! All the evidence I need to put a stop to this.'

'What? But I thought...'

'That I had become one of them?' She laughed. 'So did they.' 'I'm so sorry,' she said, reaching out to her, 'but I had to keep up the pretence. I couldn't talk to you. God, I so wanted to, but this place has ears.'

'Ears?'

Helen looked up, her eyes flicking across the walls and over the ceiling. 'They listen in. We're being bugged, day and night. Our rooms, the corridors, the... Jenny, will you stop shaking?'

'Sorry, yes, sorry.' Her eyes flitted from one corner of the room to the other. 'Can they see us? What the hell's going on?'

'No, they can't see us,' she said, 'at least I don't think they can. And I'm pretty sure they don't have this room monitored;

I've checked. But Jenny, they're all in on it. Kirkby has been carrying out experiments with the patients, injecting them, brainwashing them. He even tried it on me – he thinks he succeeded, too. Christ,' she said, grasping Jenny's hands, 'I can't even begin to tell you what's been happening, but please, I need your help. We have to...'

'Slow down! Jenny said. 'Whatever it is you need, I'm there, okay?'

Helen nodded, her stomach in knots. 'The professor...he needs to think I'm on his side. He can't know that I've spoken to you, that...'

'Helen, I get it. I do,' she interrupted. 'So we'll leave here, right? With...with...'

'A clean sheet for starters,' Helen said, pulling it from the pile and thrusting it towards her. 'And you'll change the sheet, and you won't talk to me, you *mustn't* talk to me, Jenny, and then I'll finish my shift and go back to my room. I'm leaving for London later tonight. He has to be stopped, he's completely mad, he's insane; they all are.'

Jenny gasped. 'My God.'

'I'll leave as soon as I've packed and then I'll get help. In the meantime, you have to act as if you know nothing. Can you do that?'

Jenny nodded, her eyes wide with fear.

'Jenny! You know *nothing,* do you understand?'

'Nothing,' she replied, unblinking.

'Right, then go!' Helen opened the door and shoved Jenny into the corridor, watching as she stumbled over her shoes. 'Please make sure this doesn't happen again,' she yelled, as she watched Jenny amble towards the ward, the white cotton sheet gripped firmly against her chest.

The experiments on Maria were nothing less than sadistic games carried out to feed the needs of a monster. It was all Helen could have done to stay calm and see it through to the end, without allowing him and the sister to see her revulsion. Somehow though, she'd managed.

After leaving Jenny, and as she made her way back to her room, she wondered how many minds the professor had destroyed over the years and how had he managed to get away with it for so long. These were questions that the authorities would have to investigate once he and the others involved had been brought to justice.

Aware that her room was bugged and that she was undoubtedly being monitored, she packed her belongings as quietly as she could, her thoughts turning to Mary. Why else would the hospital need overnight security in the reception area – an area that the patients had no access to and no one ever visited? It was obvious that she, along with the other receptionists, were employed to monitor the staff, to ensure nothing "untoward" was taking place. She felt sick: sick at the thought of being under surveillance; sick at what she had witnessed; sick at the depravity and inhuman behaviour by those trusted to care for their patients. But she was relieved to be leaving and to be bringing the authorities down on these awful people once and for all.

She took two of her cases to her door and then returned to her bedroom for a final check. Picking up a hold-all from her bed and slinging it over her shoulder, she took one last glance around the room and flicked off the light.

'Going somewhere, Helen?'

She spun around and looked straight into the eyes of Professor Kirkby. Sister Thornton, standing next to him, grinned at her, her eyes narrowed.

'You kept up the act up very well,' he said, 'but now, I'm afraid, the game is over.'

'Game?' Helen said, securing the bag on her shoulder. 'There is no game, Professor, I...'

'Going on holiday, are we?' He glanced down at the cases on the floor and chuckled. 'You never fooled me for a moment, my dear. '

'You can't keep me here,' Helen blurted out. 'I've informed the authorities about you; about what's going on here. They'll come looking for me.'

The professor laughed. 'Helen. You've told no one. Well, no one outside of the hospital grounds. No one will come for you.'

'You're wrong,' she said, stepping towards him. 'I've spoken to my friend, she knows I'm here, she knows...'

'Ah, the lovely Mel. Such a sweet girl.' He turned to the sister. 'How is she settling in?'

'Perfectly,' the sister said. She'll be right at home in no time.

Helen dropped her bag and thumped her fist against the wall. 'What the fuck have you done? What the *fuck*..'

'Now, now,' the professor said. 'There's no need for this outburst, Helen.' He walked slowly towards her. 'Come on, just calm down.' He glanced over his shoulder and nodded.

'Sister?'

Sister Thornton's grin widened as Jenny appeared at the door, sullen faced, pushing an empty wheelchair. She glanced briefly at Helen before preparing the restraining straps.

'You can't keep me here!' Helen yelled, backing herself into the bedroom. 'Jenny! Do something!' The back of her knees hit the base of the bed and she stumbled, falling onto the mattress. 'Jenny, run!'

The professor's chuckle echoed around the room. 'Jenny has been working with us for some time now,' he said, beckoning her in. 'She's quite the actress, don't you think? That, as they say, is how the cookie crumbles I'm afraid, Helen.'

Helen's eyes darted to the bedroom door where Jenny stood with the wheelchair, her once bright blue eyes as flat as the magnolia walls around her. She flicked her eyes back to the professor as she edged backwards up the bed. 'What are you going to do to me?' she said, her voice nothing more than a whisper.

As Jenny and the sister grasped each of her arms, Kate appeared, she and the professor smiled at each other. It was the first, proper smile Helen had ever seen on his face.

'We start, and end, with questions,' he said. 'There is no learning, no knowledge, no wisdom, without them. So tell me,' he said, because I'm desperate to know. 'What is your fear?'

The End

Other titles by this author.

Jack Preston and The Undiscovered Country

The Deadliest Game

Miranda's Fortune

The Reaping

The Cuckoo Club

www.hejoyce.com

Printed in Great Britain
by Amazon

59948460R00085